Lost in the Shadows

One Memory, Two Loves

ALAN M. OBERDECK

Cover Image: Matt Hearnea on Unsplash

Inquiries and Book Orders should be addressed to:

Great Writers Media
Email: info@greatwritersmedia.com
Phone: (302) 918-5570
16192 Coastal Highway, Lewes DE 19958, USA

ISBN: 978-1-960939-94-4 (sc)
ISBN: 978-1-960939-95-1 (eb)

"With warmth and sensitivity, the author helps us uncover the depths of feeling and levels of frustration of John, Katy and Susan. These characters live their faith in quiet, yet powerful ways; even when it might bring them pain. Don't be surprised if you find people you know within these pages."

Rev. John W. Oberdeck, PhD
Professor of Theology, emeritus
Concordia University Wisconsin

PREFACE

In all my travels I have come across places that have for some reason or another held an attraction for me. Naturally, I have an attraction to the area in Southern Wisconsin where I was born. Another one in particular is West Virginia. Many years ago, on a sales trip, I crossed Mystery Mountain and came into an area that really impressed me. The people were warm and friendly and the town was scenic, nestled in a river valley with a railroad running through it. The town was Williamson, West Virginia.

With this book, I want to tell two love stories intertwined together in such a way as the unintended consequence of one led to the other. I wanted to show the way of life in the 1960s, how people of faith approached life in that era and to illuminate some of the problems young Christian lovers faced. In this book, I have tried to be as historically accurate as possible.

I chose Williamson, West Virginia because of the people living there and the scenery of the mountains. It was the perfect place to bring John and Susan together. Yet, Henry and Katy were prototypical of many young dating couples and the religious problems faced in the 1960s. I chose a mystery as the vehicle to advance the story. I used fire in a very unusual way. You may recognize parts of many of the characters portrayed in the book as people you have known. I have tried to pattern the human nature and actions of the many Christian people I have known.

The road and the curve on Mystery Mountain is an actual place and can be reached by following the route taken in the story.

CHAPTER 1

The storm was fierce, the cold rain was coming down in buckets, and every now and then there was a strong gust of wind. Hank felt the old cabin shake with some of the harder gusts even though his cabin was sheltered by the tall trees and the mountain behind it. It was late in the evening when his dog began to whine and went to sit in front of the door. Since his wife died, Hank lived alone with Old Blue, his dog and constant companion. Old Blue usually settled down by nine or nine thirty. but he had been fidgeting all evening. It was almost eleven when he was at the door trying to get out. Hank thought it must be the storm that had Old Blue so skittish, but he never liked going out in the rain, so something must be wrong out there to excite Old Blue. He decided to check outside for whatever was causing Old Blue to act this way. His dog usually only acted this way if something out there was really wrong.

Hank lived on Rockhouse Fork Road, which is the road connecting Delbarton on the west side of Mystery Mountain to Barnabus on the east side. His cabin was located right at the base of the mountain up from the little village of Ragland. He always had been a loner, but to please his wife he had lived in town all the years he worked on the railroad. They had no children so when his wife died he was all alone, well not quite, he did have a nephew who had a family in Charleston and he had been invited to come to live with them, but Charleston was just too congested. He asked around and found this cabin and moved here. This was a nice quiet area where nothing ever happened. This was the way he liked it, quiet. So when something stirred up his dog, he put on his heavy coat to go out with Old Blue and investigate.

He stepped out of the door with Old Blue at his side and stood on his porch, looking out into the dark, rainy night. The rain had knocked some of the fall leaves from the trees and there were some new-fallen limbs in his front yard, but the foliage was still thick and he was unable to make out anything from where he stood. The rain had slackened some, so he decided to follow Old Blue out into the yard. It was then he noticed a faint, reddish glow in the sky to the east. He walked out to the road to get a better view of the glow. As he looked around, he finally decided the glow came from the top of Mystery Mountain. Something must have been on fire up there.

The sheriff's office needed to know this as soon as possible. Phone service hadn't been extended to where Hank lived and the closest phone was in Delbarton, so he went into the cabin, got the keys to his old Chevy and he and Old Blue were on their way. Together, they drove the eight miles to Delbarton, where he found a phone to report what he had seen to the sheriff's department in Williamson. Hank then called the number for the volunteer fire department in Delbarton.

Hank, being the curious person he was, loaded Old Blue back into the Chevy, and headed for the top of Mystery Mountain to see if he could find anything out himself.

Mingo County, West Virginia is one of the smallest counties in the state with the county seat located in Williamson, a city with a population of around four thousand people. What distinguishes Mingo County is that it is a bituminous coal producing county. The County Seat, Williamson, is situated in the Tug River Valley on the Tug Fork of the Big Sandy River which empties into the Ohio River between Ashland, KY and Huntington, WV. The center of the city, where most of the businesses are located, is in the lowest part of the valley along the riverbank. Most of the population lives on the sides of the hills and mountains on either side of the valley. The unusual point of interest is The Coal House, a house built from square blocks of coal. To railroad men, Williamson is better known as the key Classification Yard for assembling east bound coal and freight trains for the Norfolk and Western railway system. This being coal country, the majority of the trains leaving Williamson carried coal.

The sheriff's deputy, who answered the call, looked at the map and recognized the location. This was on County Road 65, named Rockhouse Fork Road, which wound its way up the very steep side of Mystery Mountain. If he looked over the edge of that road at this particular spot, he would look almost straight down the side of the mountain. This was not a good place to fight a fire. He also was aware that the county line was right at the top of the mountain. A fire on the mountain was something that could affect both counties. The west side was Mingo County. Everything on the east side of the mountain was in Logan County. He placed a phone call to the sheriff's office in Logan County to inform them that something had happened on or near the top of Mystery Mountain that could be a potential fire in either Mingo or Logan County and needed to be looked into.

The deputy then began the process of contacting the sheriff to apprise him of the situation. Because of the seriousness of anything affecting the production of coal, the sheriff wanted to know about everything that happened in the mountains around Williamson, and this was especially true during an Election Year. This was a Friday night, one week and three days before the 1964 General Election and the sheriff was at a political rally when the news caught up to him. He immediately left the rally to go to the top of the mountain to assess the situation.

The sheriff left the rally just as the rain was tapering off in Williamson. There was no direct route to the top of Mystery Mountain so he had to drive the distance to Delbarton and then through Ragland up to the mountain top. The roads were wet and it took him almost forty-five minutes to reach his destination.

When he arrived, he found that the Delbarton volunteers headed up by Chief Danny LeMaster had things pretty much under control. The rain had finally stopped. The fire fighters from Logan County had just arrived. Their route brought them up Old Barnabus Creek Road to the top of the mountain, this was a gravel road and they had a greater distance to come. The heavy rain made it a long, slow drive up Old Barnabus Creek Road.

The sheriff found the cause of the fire to be a burning car. The car appeared to have been traveling west and failed to negotiate the very tight turn at the top of the mountain pass. It went off the road and fell down the steep side about twenty feet onto a ledge landing on its top. The car caught fire, but fortunately, because of the heavy rain, which probably caused the accident, neither the forest floor nor the foliage in the surrounding trees were badly burned. No doubt that the gas tank had ruptured or exploded and it was the burning car that caused the glow in the sky that Hank had seen earlier.

The volunteers were able to see what looked like a body lying down the mountainside below the ledge where the flaming car laid. They told the sheriff no one had been able to get down to the body yet because of the heat, but as soon as they thought it was safe, they would send a man down the steep grade to determine the best way to retrieve it.

The sheriff from Logan County arrived. The two men walked over as close to the edge of the road as was safe and looked down at the burning wreck. They both agreed there was no doubt that the wreck was on the Mingo County side of the mountain. They also agreed that were it not for the rain storm, this fire could have easily gotten out of control and become a fiery disaster. They discussed the election and the races they were in and the prospects of their each keeping their respective jobs. The Logan County sheriff, seeing that the accident wasn't in his county and everything was under control, got in his car and headed back to Logan. He was followed by the volunteer firemen from Logan County who concluded that there was no longer an emergency and there were enough Delbarton volunteers to do the job. It was now left to the Delbarton volunteers to watch the fire finally burn out.

Hank had been the first to arrive and assess the damage, so he left Delbarton before all the volunteers had assembled at the station house to mount their fire engine and be on their way. On the way home, he though about the events that had just taken place. When he first arrived at the scene, he parked his car as far out of the way as possible and left Old Blue asleep on the front seat. He walked over to the edge of the road to look at the fire, he had not been able to get close enough because of the heat to have seen the body lying farther down the mountain. He had assumed the driver had been killed and trapped in the burning car. The very thought of burning to death in a car wreck sickened him. After the fire had cooled and the fire was nothing more than flickers of flame over hot metal, he could see that further down the mountainside there was a dark shape wedged against a tree. At first he was relieved to see the body, but due to the severity of the crash and fire that followed he had not had much hope that the person could have survived.

Hank had been here when the volunteers arrived and had watched as the fire did its job. He knew he should go home and get some sleep, but he wanted to wait around to see what they were going to do about the body.

The sheriff and the firemen could see no movement from the body and thought the person was probably dead. Considering the condition of the car and the position of the body, it would be a miracle for the person to have survived. Now the question was what to do about it. Really, the Coroner should be called to make his findings, but it was late and it would take a couple of hours to get him there. The sheriff decided to send one of the firemen to work his way down the steep mountain side with a rope to haul the body up. The Coroner could come with him tomorrow and inspect the scene, but he was not going to leave the body down there overnight.

Hank stood beside the sheriff as one of the men took a rope and began climbing down toward the body. When he got to the body, he yelled up that the person was a man who was unconscious and still breathing but hurt pretty bad. What should he do?

The sheriff and Danny LeMaster discussed the options and made a plan, they would send three more men and a stretcher down to where the man was wedged against the tree. The four men would tie the injured man to the stretcher and then slowly climb up the steep mountain-side with the stretcher. When they reached the top, they would administer what first aid they could at the fire truck and then find a way to bring him down the mountain to Delbarton.

Once they reached the bottom, the four volunteers slowly untangled the injured man from the tree that had broken his fall and positioned him on the stretcher. They tied him on as best they could to that WWI surplus stretcher they carried on the fire truck. When they first started up the mountain with the stretcher, the uneven terrain and the underbrush made it difficult to keep the stretcher stable and they had trouble making forward progress. From the road where he was looking down, Hank suggested that the first man tie the rope he had taken down with him to the stretcher so he and the sheriff could pull on the rope to keep an upward pressure on the stretcher to keep them from losing ground. This was done and the stretcher was carried up the mountainside.

While two of the firemen checked the man's vital signs and the sheriff checked his pockets for identification, Hank helped the other volunteers stow the equipment used back on the fire truck. The injured man was Caucasian with blond hair. Lying on the stretcher, he looked to be at least six feet tall. He was wearing a leather motorcycle jacket over a white tee shirt with blue jeans and leather lace-up work boots. The sheriff checked through all his pockets and found no driver's license or any other form of identification. His breathing was labored and he was still unconscious.

They decided that since the rain had stopped, they would wrap the stretcher in a blanket and place it on top of the hoses on the fire truck. One of the firemen would ride beside him back down the mountain to Delbarton. There, they could get proper transportation to the hospital. Slowly, they came down the mountain. The sheriff's car led the way, followed by the fire truck, while Hank's Chevy brought up the rear.

When they reached the bottom of the mountain, Hank left the solemn procession. He and Old Blue went into the house. *What a day this turned out to be,* he thought, *first the storm and then the accident, this was just too much excitement, but at least the accident victim should survive.* He got Old Blue settled in for the night and took care of the things needed to shut down the cabin for the night and went to bed.

It was two o'clock in the morning when the sheriff and the volunteers arrived at the station house in Delbarton. The sheriff called to Williamson to get an ambulance to come to Delbarton and pick up the accident victim. He would be treated at Williamson Memorial Hospital.

It was around two thirty Saturday morning when the sheriff got back into his car and began driving back to Williamson. It had been a long day with the rally and then this accident. It was time for him to go home. As he drove, he planned in his mind the schedule for the day. He would get in the office early so he could get back up the mountain and write up the accident report; then he would visit the victim to find out any details, then off again to meet the voters before the election. The one good thing about the evening was that it was Daylight Savings Time, meaning Sunday morning he would get an extra hour of sleep. When he got home, he slipped into bed without even waking his wife.

CHAPTER 2

Saturday morning, the weather was brisk with a cloudless sky, the storm having passed in the early morning hours. The eastern sky was bright, but the sun hadn't risen above the mountain peak yet when the sheriff arrived at his office. Normally, he didn't come in to the office to work on weekends. The weekend duties were assigned to his various deputies. Due to the accident, though, he felt that his investigation of the site just couldn't wait until Monday. So there he was, surprising his staff by his presence. He checked in with the night deputy. It had been a very quiet night in the rest of the town. He checked the paperwork lying on his desk from the night before. There was nothing there that wouldn't wait until Monday. He called over to the hospital to check on the man who had the accident. No one he talked to had any information on him other than he had been admitted and was listed as being "in a guarded condition." The sheriff decided to remain in his office for a while and fill out as much of the paperwork as he could from the comfort of his desk.

The place of the Accident: *County Road 65 named Rockhouse Fork Road at the top of the mountain at the county line with Logan County where the road name becomes Old Barnabus Creek Road.*

The date of the Accident: *Friday October 23, 1964.* Time of the Accident: *Approximately 10:30 P. M.*

Weather conditions: *Storm with heavy rain.* Visibility: *Probably poor with heavy rain and wind.*

Name of person/persons reporting the Accident: _Hank Connolly._

Names of those involved: _Unknown at this time._ Describe Accident: ______________________________

By the time he left the office, the sun had risen above the mountain and was midway up in the morning sky. It was time for him to go up to the accident site and finish writing his report. He grabbed a clipboard; clipped to it the report form he had started, grabbed his measuring tape, and headed out to his car.

As he made his way through Delbarton, he passed the fire house, a garage-like building with an office attached. There, on the apron in front of the double doors, he saw the fire chief washing last night's mud from the 1939 Chevy Fire Engine. Next, he would clean the equipment used from the previous night. This meant wash it, let it dry in the sun, and fold it back on the truck in preparation for the next time it would be used.

He passed through Delbarton and turned from Eutaw Avenue on to Rockhouse Fork Road that which would lead him up the mountain to the crash site. The gravel on the surface of the road had already dried from the rain of the night before and the other effects from the rain last night had pretty much gone away. All that was left were a few small puddles. Although the rain had been heavy, it had not brought down many leaves from the hickory, maple, and oak trees that populated the mountain. The fall colors were brilliant in the morning sun. As he drove higher up the mountainside, he looked back down the steep side of the road at the valley below. Everything seemed so peaceful from where he stopped on the mountain.

As he approached the area where the accident happened, he parked, picked up his tape measure and clipboard, and exited the car. The accident happened at the very top of the mountain where a cut about thirty feet deep had been made to make the road as level as possible as it crossed the top of the mountain. The road coming west up the mountain from Barnabus passed through the cut and abruptly turned left to hug the steep western side as it made its way down to go to Delbarton. He walked the path the westbound car would have driven on the road to the top of the mountain and around the curve. He could see how easy it would have been, in the blinding rain, to miss the sign with the arrow pointing to the curve. He could see where the car turned too late at that narrow point in the road and slid sideways, toppling the barrier that had been there. He imagined what it would have looked like to see the car falling over the edge, landing on its top on the shelf below.

He measured the length of the path where the driver first went off the gravel to the point where the car left the road completely. He inspected the posts from the old barrier. They had rotted away and wouldn't have stopped a small bicycle. What was left of the barricade had probably been consumed in the fire. *If this had happened when the woods were dry*, he noted, *there would probably have been a rather large fire considering how dry the forest floor would have been*. Thankfully, the floor of the forest was already well-soaked and seemed to burn only where the gasoline had spread.

The sheriff climbed down to the narrow ledge and walked over to the burned out hulk of the car. It was an older model Ford two door coupe. From the back, it looked to be a 1949 to 1951 model. He would have to look more closely to determine the exact year. He looked at the license tag bracket in the back. He carefully walked around the car. Both the front and back brackets were empty. He went over to the left side door, which had sprung partway open during the crash. He crawled in and reached inside to get to the glove box. He was able to open it and look in. There, he found the burned remains of what appeared to be a billfold and some charred papers. Nothing in the billfold was readable; it crumbled into ash immediately when he picked it up. There were, however, several tightly folded papers in a leather binder that seemed to have survived most of the heat. He would take good care of this and open it later. As he half laid there in what was left of the car, he marveled at the fact the driver had even been able to get out. The way the door was open indicated how he might have been thrown clear of the car on the way down. This force might have been what wedged him into the tree, keeping him from falling farther down the mountainside.

He crawled back away from the right side door and circled to the front. The hood had been sprung during the fall, so he was able to peer into the engine compartment. There, he saw the Ford six-cylinder engine. Looking at the front of the hood, he could see some of the letters spelling the name FORD. That would make the car a 1949 model, since the name was replaced by the Ford emblem on the front of the hood on the 1950 models. He looked for the serial number but could not get to it. From where the car was positioned on the mountainside, it was going to be difficult to move. Then again, if no one objected and it was up to the county to move the car, it would probably just stay there and rust away.

The sheriff sat in his car and finished writing as much of the report as he could at the site. He would be able to find answers to the last questions as soon as he could visit and talk to the man in the hospital.

It was near noon when the sheriff got back to his office. He decided to go home and eat lunch with his wife. He hadn't talked to her early in the morning when he got home. When he awoke, she was already up and made him breakfast, but they hadn't had much time to talk other than his mentioning the accident. He remembered the political function they were supposed to attend tonight.

When he arrived home, he had a leisurely lunch with his wife.

"You know, I would really like to take the afternoon off and go do something with you," he said to his wife as he got up from the table to leave.

She just nodded her head knowing that the next words from his mouth would be about work.

"I should finish gathering the information on the accident last night to finish my report. I need to get his name and find out who to notify about the accident," the sheriff continued.

"Remember now we are expected to be at the meeting hall by at least 5:30 p.m. for the pig roast rally," she called to him as he was going out the door.

"This shouldn't take that long, I should be back before five," he called back.

The drive up the hill to Williamson Memorial Hospital gave the sheriff some time to think more about some of the things that bothered him about the accident.

What was that person thinking to drive up over the mountain on such a stormy night anyway? Where was he going? What happened to the license tag? Why wasn't it on the car?

On his way into the Williamson Memorial Hospital entrance, he stopped at the reception desk to say hello to Molly and glean what he could about things in general. She was a middle aged lady with graying hair, sparkling green eyes, a pleasant smile and an outgoing personality. They had known each other since high school and usually discussed grandchildren whenever he came by, as it usually took her some time to locate whomever he had come to see.

This time it was a little different, though, as the person he had come to see was the accident victim and she could find no name or information listed for him. What she found was a note. It indicated the doctor in charge wanted to see the sheriff as soon as he came in. While Molly waited for the doctor to answer his page, they talked about grandchildren.

When the doctor finally arrived, he and the sheriff walked down the hall toward the nurse's station on the first floor.

"How is the patient?" asked the sheriff.

"The patient is doing fine. He is in a bit of a fog yet over what happened, but he is conscious and able to drink something, but that is about all. We sent him up to X-ray this morning and other than a broken leg, he seems to be in pretty good shape," the doctor replied.

"Is he in any condition for me to go and talk with him now?" asked the sheriff.

"He is still pretty groggy from the sedative and you may not make much sense out of his answers, but we can see if his condition has improved," answered the doctor. "He is in room twelve."

They walked down the hall to the room and entered a typical 1960's two bed hospital room. As you entered through the door you passed by the bathroom door to where the two beds were lined up against an inside wall. Across from the door in the outer wall was a window.

The bed closest to the window was empty. The other bed had a wooden frame attached to it with a trapeze hanging down over the chest of the man laying on his back in it. He was covered with a thin white cotton blanket with only his red face, which showed signs of having been exposed to great heat, and parts of his right leg, where it was out of the covers and elevated by ropes and pulleys on the frame, showing. Much of his blond hair had been singed away in the fire and his eyebrows were almost completely gone.

"Good afternoon," said the doctor. "How are you feeling?"

"Kinda sore. My face hurts and I have pain in my right leg," answered the patient.

"That can be expected," answered the doctor. "You have some superficial burns on your face and the backs of your hands and your eye brows and some hair have been singed. The nurses have been instructed to apply Vaseline to those areas. Have they done that yet?" questioned the doctor.

"I don't remember them doing that," the patient answered.

"The X-rays from this morning show you have a broken leg. The break is a simple closed fracture, which will not need surgery. That is why you are splinted and in traction. We will have to wait until it forms a callus before it can be placed in a cast."

"How did this happen?" asked the patient.

That question took both the doctor and the sheriff by surprise. They looked at each other and the doctor shrugged.

"Do you feel well enough to talk right now?" the doctor asked.

"Sure, I guess," the patient replied.

"If you are up to it, the sheriff would like to ask you some questions and maybe answer some of yours," the doctor counseled.

"Okay," the patient answered.

"Son, the first thing I want to get from you is your name," stated the sheriff.

The patient's face showed a sudden look of confusion, followed by the look of deep concentration. After about a minute passed, he looked up at the two men standing there and answered.

"I can't remember!"

"Sometimes after a trauma, this will happen. Maybe after talking more about last night, things will clear up," reassured the doctor.

"Where is your home?" the doctor continued.

Again, the patient's face took on a very confused look before answering.

"I don't know."

"How old are you?" quizzed the doctor.

Again, after some delay, the patient hesitatingly answered.

"I don't know."

"Do you remember anything from last night?" asked the sheriff.

"Not a thing," he answered, sounding confused.

The sheriff looked at the doctor. Again, the doctor shrugged his shoulders and looked down at the floor as if in deep thought, but said nothing.

The sheriff then addressed the patient.

"Last night, in the storm, you missed the sharp curve on the top of Mystery Mountain and drove your car over the edge of a cliff. The car burned, but you either crawled or were thrown clear. You only suffered a broken leg. Does any of this bring back any memory?"

The patient looked stunned. He laid there with his confused look again on his face. He said nothing but rolled his head to the side of the bed away from the doctor and the sheriff, looking at the wall.

"I think it is time to give the patient a rest and wait until he is off the pain medication. He will probably remember a lot more then," counseled the doctor.

With that, the two men left the room and walked back down the hall to the nurse's station, discussing the next steps in his treatment. They decided to identify him by the location of his wreck, so for the record they called him John Rockhouse. That would be the name on his records until he could remember his Christian name. The doctor went over to the nurse's station to find out why no Vaseline had been applied to the patients superficial burns yet.

With that all decided, the sheriff said good-bye to Molly at the desk and left Williamson Memorial Hospital to continue his day.

John Rockhouse lay in his bed just as confused as ever, not knowing that he now had a name.

Now for the first time, he started to try to put things together in his mind. *Where was he anyway? What was his name anyway?* He looked around the room and tried to make sense of it. He realized he was in a hospital room with two beds. The walls were white, the ceiling was white. The bed had a wooden contraption on it that held his leg in traction. His nose picked up the smells he associated with being in a hospital.

The room was rectangular with a window on one wall. The window was covered with half open Venetian blinds. He couldn't see much through the window except sky and what looked like the ridge of a mountain. Under the window was what looked like an oblong box with vents on the top. *This must be the heater for the room*, he reasoned. Between his bed and the window was another bed, definitely a hospital bed. It was empty. Beside each of the beds was a night stand with a drawer under the top and a door under that. There was also a stand that could be rolled up to the bed to form a bed table. At this point, it was rolled off to the side. At the end of the beds were two lounge type chairs. He figured those were for the visitors that would come to keep someone company.

"*Where am I*?" he asked himself.

He listened for what he could hear. The normal sounds he attributed to a hospital were present: the sounds of feet hitting the floor out in the hall as they walked by the door to his room, the sound of metal dishes occasionally clanging as they were bumped together, and the faint sound of a radio somewhere down the hall.

Then, when these quieted down, he recognized the horn from a diesel locomotive, and when it was real quiet outside, the screeching of the rail car wheels as they rounded a curve.

He had no answer for where he was, didn't know his name, was tired, confused, frustrated, lonely and needed sleep. Yet, from somewhere deep inside came the desire to fold his hands and pray. "Now I lay me down to sleep…" and during this prayer he drifted off to sleep.

CHAPTER 3

Sunday found John Rockhouse laying painfully on his bed in traction. His right leg was elevated and he had pins and other things sticking out of the skin of his thigh. Either the pain was greater than the painkillers could handle or the drugs had worn off. In any case, he needed another shot.

Not only could he not move wherever he wanted to, but his skin felt sore and tender around the pins. The nurses woke him early so he could eat a small breakfast. Now nature was calling, so he was waiting on the nurse to bring him the proper equipment. *How am I going to do this?* he thought, *I'm on my back, can't move and hanging from this contraption. I feel totally helpless!*

He still had no memory of who he was or what had happened to put him here. No one had told him yet that he was now called John Rockhouse, so when that name was used by the nurses in his presence he was confused.

While he was waiting for the doctor to visit him this morning, he really tried to get things straight in his mind. Yesterday, they had a lot of questions for him. He was somewhat groggy and only halfway remembered what they had been saying. This morning, he was much more alert and full of questions that needed answers.

Not far away, the sheriff had awakened from a sound sleep, troubled by the circumstances of the patient, John Rockhouse, and the accident.

Late at night or early in the morning, as in this case, was the time when he did his best thinking. Unfortunately, over the years, it had also cost him some of his best sleep time. The circumstances of the accident were obvious. The details that surrounded the accident bothered him: the person had no name or identification, the person was dressed in motorcycle attire, the car had no tag or identification, and the person was unable to remember his name or where he was from. There were just too many details that did not add up. Then the sheriff's mind began to extrapolate on what he knew, as happens when one awakens during the night, and he began to imagine possibilities. *Was this man a crook? Could he have stolen that car? Was he on the run from the law? Was he faking the memory loss to avoid detection? Was he a danger to the community? Of course, in his current condition he couldn't do much harm to the community. Did he have insurance to cover this? This was now a county problem. Who was going to pay for his recuperation? Was the county liable in a case like this? Obviously, the hospital couldn't absorb the cost. Would it come out of his department budget?*

These were the types of questions keeping him awake in the early morning hours on this Sunday when he had planned to get that needed extra hour of sleep.

The doctor made his morning rounds at Williamson Memorial Hospital a little after noon. Things can get hectic on a Sunday morning with church and the family taking up more time than originally expected. He knocked on the door and he and a nurse entered room twelve.

"Good afternoon," he opened.

"Good afternoon," replied John Rockhouse.

The doctor picked up the chart hanging on the foot of the bed and studied it for a moment, then handed it to the nurse. The vital signs looked good. There was a little fever, but that was expected.

"Everything on your chart looks good. How do you feel?" he asked.

"I hurt a lot and I itch under the tape," came the reply.

"The pain will gradually become less, but the itching is just something you will have to put up with while the bone heals," the doctor said knowingly. "Let me check those dressings to make sure the tape is not causing irritation." The doctor peeled away the tape.

"How long will I be here?" the patient asked.

"That depends on how fast you heal. Normally, the leg will be in traction for about six weeks, then you will be in the cast for about six months, then you should be healed. The cast will be from your hip to your toes, but you will be able to get around in a wheelchair and on crutches," he stated.

"Can you answer some questions that are bothering me?" the patient inquired.

"What do you want to know?" the doctor responded.

"Where am I? What day is this? And who is this John Rockhouse the nurses are talking about?" he asked.

"Well, let's see what I can do to answer all your questions," the doctor answered with a smile on his face. "First, today is Sunday, October 25th, 1964. You are in Williamson Memorial Hospital in Williamson, West Virginia. The last question you asked is one that we should have explained to you yesterday before the sheriff and I left the building. Have you remembered your name yet?"

"No, and that is another thing I want to ask you about," came the reply.

"Let's clear up the John Rockhouse thing first. Your accident took place on the top of Mystery Mountain on Old Rockhouse Road. Yesterday, when you couldn't remember your name, the sheriff and I needed a name for your charts and his reports. We didn't want to use the John Doe name as that is usually applied to unidentified dead bodies. We then decided to use a name identified with your accident site, thus John Rockhouse. I had hoped that by today you would have remembered your Christian name. Is the name okay with you?" the doctor asked.

"Yeah, I guess that is better than John Doe," he declared.

"Now, to answer the question of your memory, what you have is a form of amnesia. Amnesia is defined as profound memory loss. It can happen after an accident and if it is related to a hard blow to the head, generally is transient, which means that it usually goes away after a short period of time. Now, we will just have to wait and see what you begin to remember. I wouldn't worry about it," was the answer the doctor gave. "If you have no more questions, I will leave you in the care of the lovely nurses here at the hospital and see you tomorrow. Nurse, when you put the dressing back, try crossing the tape this way so it doesn't put pressure on the tender part of the skin."

With that statement, the doctor turned and left John Rockhouse alone in his bed in traction in his sterile, white, lonely room.

Unknown to John Rockhouse, however, the doctor had quite a lot on his mind. He had never before witnessed a case of amnesia. From all his medical experience and his current reading, it appeared amnesia was very rare. He questioned whether this was even real, yet John showed every sign of being sincere. In any case, much study would have to be put into the case of John Rockhouse.

The sheriff spent the day on the campaign trail, but couldn't concentrate fully on the people with whom he was shaking hands. There were still so many questions hovering around the accident. He decided that in the morning this would be his first priority.

John Rockhouse spent a fitful night in bed trying to become comfortable lying on his back in this strange position. He was looking up at the wooden frame attached to the head and the foot of his bed, to which pulleys, wires, and weights were attached. Most of the pain medicine had worn off and he was just thinking and wondering what had put him here. He tried to remember, but all that was there was a big, confusing void. As hard as he tried, he could not penetrate the vacuum of that void.

He laid there in bed listening to the sounds in the night, trying to identify what he was hearing. There were the faint noises of the hospital routines echoing up and down the hall: a slammed door, the buzz of quiet voices, and the metal clatter of what must have been a bed pan. Occasionally, he would hear the noise from the railroad: the horn of a railroad engine at a crossing and the squeal of railroad car wheels rounding a curve.

Finally, from somewhere deep in his mind came a prayer: *Now I lay me down to sleep I pray the Lord my soul to keep*, and blessed sleep followed.

CHAPTER 4

The sheriff got up early Monday morning, ate the breakfast his patient wife had prepared, kissed her good-bye, and headed to his office early. The sky was clear and now that Daylight Savings Time had gone, the sun was clearing the mountain by the time he got to the office. He already knew what was on the agenda from Saturday. He hoped Sunday had been quiet and that there were not many things needing his immediate attention.

He checked in with the deputy at the front desk and made his way back to his cluttered desk. His wish had been answered. Sunday had been a quiet day around the county. Now to finish his report on Friday night's accident.

Names of those involved: *Unknown at this time as the driver appears to be suffering from amnesia.*

Describe Accident: *Driver drove off the edge of the mountain at the county line between Logan and Mingo at the point where Old Barnabus Road changes to Old Rockhouse Road. The car went down the mountainside, landing on its roof on a ledge. The ensuing fire destroyed the car.*

He concluded with the description of the accident and completed the report. Now he decided he must investigate the driver.

Was the car stolen? Was that the reason there wasn't a license tag on the car? He began to call around to the counties close to Mingo to see if there had been any old Ford cars stolen. There were stolen cars reported, but none of them were 1949 Ford two door coupes. *Was the driver a fugitive?* He checked for any current fugitive warrants. There were warrants that had come across his desk, but none of them fit the description of the man lying in a bed at Williamson Memorial Hospital.

In any case, he concluded, if John Rockhouse was a fleeing criminal, he would be no threat to the community in his condition in the hospital. The sheriff made still more phone calls trying to identify John and left word with a number of people to call him back if they found out anything. The sheriff placed another visit to the hospital on his schedule for that afternoon. He then went on to handle the routine Monday morning things that happened around his office.

Back at the hospital, the doctor was preparing for the rounds he would be making this morning. They didn't schedule surgeries on Mondays to give the staff time to clean up from whatever mayhem had happened over the weekend. Usually, they had the normal Saturday night auto accident to attend to, the children with broken arms and legs from the sports activities that they pursued over the weekend, the older people with breathing problems that had to be admitted, and a range of other irregular problems. This past weekend had seen fewer than normal occurrences of disaster and disease, which translated into time for him to study up on amnesia. Medical school was long ago and he didn't remember much that was taught about amnesia, so it was hit the books to find out what treatments are available for John Rockhouse.

His reading classified amnesia into three general types. Antegrade is when a person can't retain any new memories. This usually occurs after an injury to the brain. Retrograde is linked to a trauma, after which the patient loses memories of things previous to his current state. The third is Transient Global Amnesia, which lasts for a short time, but leaves one unable to remember past events.

There are a number of subclasses of amnesia which can fall under the main three, but these are related to specific known cases. The real problem comes down to how to treat these symptoms.

His conclusions from what he was reading were: this memory loss was probably due to a blow to the head during the accident, which would place this in the category of Retrograde Amnesia. If there was damage to the brain and he lost brain cells, he may never get some of the memories back. On the other hand, this could repair itself and he could remember most of what he lost.

The only way to treat Retrograde Amnesia would be through time and observation. According to what he read, the patient should be remembering more and more things as time goes by. One of the suggested treatments would be to take him back to familiar surroundings with the thought that familiar sites will trigger memories. For this particular patient, treatment will be possible when he remembers more and his injuries have healed, the doctor concluded. But for the time being, he would remain in the hospital and not move.

Now, the big question would be how to get the time to evaluate the extent of the memory loss. The doctor decided that the best approach would be to have him do some type of mental work while he was unable to leave the hospital. The types of things he would be able to do would be based on arithmetic, sorting, and interacting with him. On his rounds, he would take time to do his initial evaluation.

John was awakened around six thirty by the nurse taking his vital signs. He still felt sleepy, but the buzz of activity taking place in the hall was enough stimulation to keep him awake and staring at the bed frame above him and the various shadows on the ceiling above. He felt gnawing in the stomach, which meant breakfast time should be near. He could hear the clattering of the trays in the hall, which increased the speed at which his stomach acids built up in anticipation of the meal. What a let down when the tray arrived! He got a small glass of juice, a half slice of buttered toast, a carton of milk, and a dab of oatmeal in a bowl. At least the nurse had a friendly face!

His night had been restful once he had fallen asleep and his pain was less today. The position he was in was still not comfortable, but it was becoming more and more bearable. At this point, all he could do was to sleep and wait for the doctor to pay his promised visit. Of course, the nurses came and went from his room. First was the sponge bath. This was a very awkward time, as he was very modest and the nurse was trying to wash where no man dared to go. Then there was the changing of the linen, which was quite some feat considering how his leg was trussed. Naturally, during the middle of all this, nature called and the whole thing was disrupted by the bedpan drill. John learned to love that trapeze that hung from the framework above his bed as it allowed him to raise himself from the mattress to use the bedpan.

He dozed until lunch time, when he was awakened for the meal. He was expecting this to be as dismal and sparse as breakfast, but was pleasantly surprised by the amount of food he was given. It wasn't tasty as tasty goes, but it felt good in the stomach and that was what really counted.

It was around three when the doctor and the nurse holding his chart came into his room.

"How was your night, John?" asked the doctor, hoping that he would reply with a statement something like, *"Actually, my name is Ralph or Joe.*

"Once I got to sleep, my night went pretty good. They did wake me pretty early, though," John answered.

"We have them do that on purpose around here. We don't want the patients to get the idea that this is some kind of leisure resort," replied the doctor with a grin. "In any case, I see from your chart that your fever is down and you are eating. These are all good signs."

"I guess that should make me feel good. Did I hear you right yesterday that I will be here in this bed trussed up like this for six weeks?"

"That is about how long it will take for the leg to knit so we can place it in a cast," replied the doctor.

"I am still confused. Do you have any answers for that yet?"

"That will still take time, but I don't know just how long. Nurse, get the tray over here. I want to look at his dressings."

The doctor proceeded to remove the dressings and inspect the area around the pins.

"Nurse, I am going to leave the dressings off. Instead, clean the pins in the morning and in the evening with peroxide and continue with the Vaseline on his burns.

Then the doctor addressed John again.

"John, I don't want you to get too bored laying around here all day, so I have brought you a pencil, an eraser, and a book of crossword puzzles to work through. I think it will be good therapy and may help you remember some things. Do you think you can do that?"

"Yeah, I will try my best!"

"Very good. I will be around again tomorrow to see how you do."

With that, he and the nurse exited the room.

A short time passed and the nurse came back and cleaned around the area where the pins came through the skin on his leg. She then draped a sheet around the leg to keep it warm.

When she left, he picked up the crossword puzzle book and began to read the questions. This would certainly take up his time trying to fill in the blanks. He picked up his pencil and began. 1. Across, a three letter word used to describe frozen water. *That world be ice.* 1. Down, describes a place where it would be hard for a man to survive.

Yeah, he thought, *working a crossword puzzle should keep my mind busy.*

Downtown, another mind was busy too. By mid afternoon, the sheriff had still not had any response to his earlier inquiries and decided he would go up to the hospital and see what he could learn from John Rockhouse. His strategy was going to be to try to get to know John on a friendly basis rather than try to interrogate him to get as much information from him as possible, just because there weren't any wanted posters for John yet didn't mean there wouldn't be any later.

When he got to the hospital, he found Molly had the day off and the lady at the desk had no notes or other information for him. He went right to room twelve to talk to John Rockhouse.

He knocked on the door and entered the room.

"Good afternoon, John."

"Good afternoon."

"How are you finding your stay in the hospital?

"Okay, I guess," as he turned his head toward the sheriff and smiled.

"Have you remembered anything more about the accident since yesterday?

"No, I haven't remembered anything, but the doctor has given me a crossword puzzle to see if working that will help me gain my memory back sooner."

"Well, I wanted to come by and talk to you about what I am trying to do to help. So far, I have been calling around to find out if anyone has reported you missing. So far, no one in this area has reported you or your car missing."

"Is that good or bad?"

"I guess that depends on your point of view. Nobody is looking to arrest you. On the other hand, nobody as of yet is concerned about your whereabouts either. So I guess that is both good and bad news. I had hoped you would have remembered something more."

"I guess I like the good news part," John replied.

The sheriff got a serious look on his face and looked John straight in the eye as he asked, "Have you any idea why you tried to cross Mystery Mountain in such a rainstorm? What was going through your mind?"

John got that very confused look again on his face and hesitated holding his hand on his head as if in pain and frustratingly answered.

"I only wish I could remember."

"Well, I guess I should leave you to practice the crossword puzzles then to see if they help," said the sheriff.

"Yeah, maybe this crossword puzzle will help. So far, I have been able to remember the answers to a lot of the questions, but I need so much help on them."

"Well, I will leave you to your work then and get back to mine," said the sheriff as he headed for the door.

John felt exhausted after the sheriff left. He had been thinking hard on the questions from the crossword puzzle, and trying to remember for the sheriff really wore him out. He relaxed and within moments he was laying there on his back fast asleep.

He awoke to a cheery voice. This voice sounded like one from somewhere deep in a memory he could not quite retrieve. It was the way she spoke that sounded so familiar.

"Hello, sleepyhead. It is time for you to eat your supper," she said as she placed the tray on the bedside tray table.

John looked at a young nurse in a white uniform with a starched white cap on her head that was decidedly different than the ones the other nurses wore. She was tall and of a husky build with honey blond hair. It was the blue of her eyes and the smile on her face that somehow evoked a familiarity deep inside him, as though he should know her. He stared at her name tag. It was no help. He read Miss Radke, RN.

"Uh, thanks."

She pushed the tray table over the bed where he could reach it and helped place his pillows as he lifted himself to a more sitting position.

"There," she said. "That should make it easier for you to eat."

"Thank you," John answered as she turned and left the room to deliver the next tray to the next patient.

What just happened? John wondered as he began to eat his dinner meal. *Nurse Radke*, he thought. *Why did she sound so familiar?*

Nurse Radke came back later and picked up his tray, checked his vital signs, and gave him his evening pills.

Again, he lay for a long time listening to the background hospital noise until the activity in the hall lessened and the whole floor became very quiet. Again, he could faintly hear the sounds of the trains.

Finally, he felt the drowsiness that accompanied sleep and a prayer came to his mind. His prayer completed, he fell asleep.

CHAPTER 5

Tuesday morning found the sheriff in his office completing the necessary paperwork from the Friday night accident at the top of the mountain. He had gathered all his notes to add to the official report when he spotted the charred leather item that looked to be a document holder or "wallet." It was laying on his desk beneath the clipboard he had used on Saturday when he had inspected the accident. He remembered having pulled it from the glove box in the car, but never inspecting it. It had been the only thing that had not crumbled to ash when he touched it. It was still in one piece, but very brittle.

Carefully, he unfolded it, trying not to cause the leather to break away at the folds. As he worked at it, the edges crumbled away, but what was left inside was an almost carbonized piece of paper. The only things readable were the words printed toward the center in the body of the letter. He looked carefully at what could be seen of the document as he opened the document holder. The words he could make out were "Bill of Sale," "ord 194," and "ter 17, 1964." He studied what was left of the piece of paper. From what he could make out, he concluded it recorded the sale of a "Ford 1949" bought "October 17, 1964."

There were other words he could make out, but they made no sense, so he judged them not to be relevant. This solved his question about the lack of a license tag. The car had been recently bought. Either the tag had not been applied for yet, or if it had, there had not been enough time for the tag to be sent or for the buyer receive it. This was definitely a clue that would give him a place to begin to look. If this transaction had taken place in West Virginia, he might be able to trace it through the Motor Vehicle Department in Charleston.

He immediately placed a call to a friend at the Motor Vehicle Department to see if the sale could be traced. His friend told him that it would probably take several weeks. There probably were very few 1949 Ford cars sold used in the past six weeks, but if there had been, the probability of finding out the man's name should be pretty good.

One thing was sure now, though. The car wasn't stolen, but that still didn't mean John wasn't running from something else.

Back at the hospital, John was still getting used to the routine of early to rise and wait. Something had happened late yesterday afternoon that had given him some hope. He had stirrings in the back of his mind when that nurse had brought him supper. He had also made some progress on a number of the crossword puzzle lines. John just couldn't wait to tell the doctor what good things were happening.

He spent most of the morning as he had the day before, waiting for the visit by the doctor. He worked on the crossword puzzle and was remembering a lot of words. He wondered if having a dictionary would help him in his remembering. In any case, he was feeling very optimistic about his progress.

Sometime after lunch, he wasn't sure of the time, the sheriff knocked on his door and walked in.

"Hello, John."

"Hi."

"It sure is a pretty day out there with all the fall colors," said the sheriff, trying to make small talk to put John at ease.

"I can't see much of anything from this position in the bed. Mostly, I see sky and the mountain ridge. As you can see, I can't change my position in this bed much to get a better view, the way I am roped up," John answered in a joking manner.

"Have you remembered anything more since yesterday?"

"Yeah, I think I have been doing pretty good answering the lines on this crossword puzzle," he answered confidently.

"Do you have any memories of a fire?"

"No."

"When I was up at the car, I found something that was not totally burned in the crash. I want to ask you about it. It might be something you can identify."

"I'll do my best. Do you have it here?"

At this point, the sheriff showed John the charred leather *wallet* where the bill of sale had been found.

"Can you identify this?" the sheriff asked as he handed it to John.

John turned the charred leather wallet around in his hands thoroughly inspecting it.

"It seems like I should know what that is, but I can't tell you what it is. It just looks—I don't know!" The confusion that filled his face echoed through in his voice.

"I found this in the glove box of the car. Everything else was burned beyond recognition. A small scrap of paper was folded in this. This might be a way of finding your identity."

"What was on the paper?" John asked excitedly.

"It was a bill of sale, but the names and other important bits of information were so charred no other information could be read. I had hoped that you could identify the wallet. As it is, I have put in a call to the State Motor Vehicle Department to see if they can find the paperwork on the license tag application. This should help us find out who you are and where you came from.

"Yeah, that is really good news!"

"That's about all I have come up with, but I wanted to see if it could help you remember. I will get back to you when I know more," said the sheriff as he left the room and headed down the hall. The sheriff left a note for the doctor with Molly at the desk and headed back to his office.

It was some time before the doctor finally made his rounds and came in to visit John.

"Good afternoon, John," said the doctor as he and the nurse entered the room.

"Good afternoon."

He came over to the bed and picked the chart off the hook at the end of the bed where it hung and studied it. He handed the chart to the nurse and went over to the side of the bed to inspect the leg. "How are you feeling?"

"Pretty good."

"Are the pins bothering you anymore?"

"No."

"Are you having any pain in the leg?"

"Maybe a little when I move a certain way, but I am careful and it doesn't give me any problems.

"Let me just check the pins again today and see that the redness is going away." With that, the doctor lifted the sheet that was draped over the leg and looked at the place where the pins came through the skin.

"These look very good," he said to the nurse, "but continue with the peroxide cleaning twice a day".

"Well, it looks like you are behaving yourself," he said to John.

"Been doing my best."

"Now for the big question of the day. How are you doing with the crossword puzzles?"

"I think I'm doing pretty well. I can get the answers to most of the questions, but it would really help to have a dictionary. I think I could find some of the words that have a few letters in them which would give me the answers to some of the questions."

The doctor answered, "I think that can be arranged. Nurse, there should be one in the reading room you can get for him later."

"Have you been able to remember any more details of the crash or before?

"The sheriff was in to see me earlier and he had what he called a wallet that seemed familiar to me, but I couldn't bring any memories back. I was dozing yesterday when the evening nurse came in. I think here name was Nurse Radke. Anyway, as I was waking up, I thought I was hearing someone from home, and I thought I should know her, but when I saw her, I knew it had been mistake."

"What about her did you notice?"

"I heard her voice and the way she talked seemed to remind me of someplace where people talk like that. It felt very comforting."

"None of the other nurses talk this way, then?" the doctor asked.

"Not that I have heard."

"Nurse, do you know this Nurse Radke?"

"I know most of the nurses on all three shifts. I believe she was a new hire this fall. I think she was fresh out of school, someplace in the Midwest," answered the nurse.

"Anything else you remember?" the doctor asked John.

"Nothing else."

The doctor turned to the nurse and said, "His face and hands are looking better you can stop using the Vaseline and don't cover the leg with the sheet for a while. Leave it open to the air until after the evening peroxide cleaning. I think leaving it open to the air will do it some good."

With that, the doctor turned and made his way to the door. He was followed by the nurse who hung John's chart back on the hook at the end of the bed.

The doctor stopped by Molly's desk.

"Has the sheriff been by to see John Rockhouse today?"

"Why, yes," Molly answered. "And he left you a note. Here it is." She handed him the note, which he shoved into the pocket of his white lab coat to be read later.

Later that afternoon, a nurse brought a massive dictionary to John's room and laid it on his bedside table. He had to use both hands to hold it when he wanted to look up anything, but he found that if he knew several letters to a word that he didn't know, he could, with patience, find a word that would fit a specific blank. In this way, he began to make sense of the crossword puzzle he was working on.

Later still, the nurse came back and cleaned his pins and re-draped the sheet over his leg.

John waited for supper to be served so he could again hear Nurse Radke talk. Unfortunately, it was another nurse who took care of him this night. Nurse Radke must have been making the rounds in another section.

CHAPTER 6

Four weeks had passed and John Rockhouse was in poor spirits as he lay in bed on his back he began to think, *Thanksgiving is just a few days away, what is it that I have to be thankful for anyway? Well at least I lived through the accident, I am thankful for that. I can't even remember my name or where I came from. Remembering that would be something to be really thankful for. Am I making progress? I can't remember anything more than I remembered the last time the sheriff was here, but I have been doing better with my crossword puzzles.*

The sheriff had just been by to visit him with the latest news. First and foremost, the sheriff announced he had been re-elected and reassured John that he would continue to work on this case. The sheriff then told him what he had found so far in his investigation. The long and the short of it was that the State of West Virginia Motor Vehicle Department had not been able to find any record of the sale or request for a tag for the 1949 Ford Coupe. Just to be thorough, the sheriff had also contacted the neighboring states of Virginia, Kentucky, Ohio, Pennsylvania, and Maryland with no success. The car was so old that few people had bought or sold that model of Ford car in the last three months. So much luck for finding his name from the purchase of the car. The result: he was back to square one.

John was still working on the empty spaces in the crossword puzzles. They needed the big dictionary back in the reading room, so he had lost that. He was now in the habit of asking the nurses for help with some of the words when they came in to take care of him. The questions made good conversation as there was nothing else he really could talk about with them anyway. He was in a double room but the other bed had been empty when he arrived and the hospital census was such that they never filled that bed. He could hear a radio down the hall in another room, but it wasn't loud enough for him to understand what programs were on. If he had had any friends or relatives, he would have had them bring him a radio or even some current magazines. If only they would fill the empty bed, he would have someone to talk to and maybe that person would have a radio.

On some nights, Nurse Radke would be the nurse taking care of him. He so much looked forward to the times when she was there. She used words that touched some parts of his memory such as "beer" and "knackwurst." Over the weeks, through observation and so many conversations with her, he had learned some things about her. She was tall, almost six feet was his guess. He couldn't tell exactly, lying in bed as he was, but that was his best guess. Her hair wasn't blond exactly, but it wasn't brown either. It was more the color of honey. She wore it in what could be called a pageboy cut, which looked good under the white nurse's hat. Her blue gray eyes could burn holes through you if you were on her bad side. She had the most pleasant smile when she was pleased. She usually wore white uniforms with a full skirt. Her figure was right out of the lingerie section of the Sears and Roebuck Catalog. You could say *model perfect.*

She grew up in Wisconsin John came to find out. *She* had lived in a little town called Milton. *She* spent three years in Milwaukee going to school. This fall, she graduated from Milwaukee Hospital School of Nursing. *She* had never been far from the greater Wisconsin area and when she graduated, *she* wanted to see the world. *She* considered going into the Army, but her family was against that, so she looked at going out of state. Williamson Memorial Hospital had caught her attention from an advertisement they ran about life in the "Beautiful Tug River Valley." *She* became fascinated with the area and pursued it. The small town she came from was situated at the edge of a glacial moraine and, except for a few hills, was essentially flat. Williamson, on the other hand, was a small town located in a valley surrounded by mountains. The mountains appealed to her and, although this wasn't the highest paid offer she looked at, she chose this one because of the scenery and the people she met here.

Nurse Radke was always very professional with him and he never called her by her first name. Yet, of all the nurses that cared for him, she was the friendliest. She would joke with him. She would tell him what the Green Bay Packers were doing. He heard about Bart Star and Paul Horning. She never stayed long, but she was always cheerful and had some funny remark to make. She stirred a deep, far off feeling of a home, wherever that was.

For the doctor, John Rockhouse was the great mystery to be unraveled. The greatest medical challenge he had encountered in his practice so far. To unravel this one was the challenge that kept him studying about amnesia. He had to find the answers to the basic questions: who is he, where did he come from, how old is he, and what caused his loss of memory?

The doctor was still watching John for signs that his memory was returning. He was also noticing other things about him. He couldn't spend as much time as he wanted with John, but the time he did spend was leading to some very interesting observations.

John definitely was not originally from this area. His speech patterns seemed to be more Midwest. That would place him definitely west of Ohio, north of Kentucky, Southern Indiana, Southern Illinois, and Missouri. That left a lot of area he could be from.

John used some interesting sentence structures, such as placing the noun, the verb, and the adjective out of order. He had heard this before in the English speech pattern of some Amish farmers when he had been visiting in Pennsylvania, but the speech pattern was not from that area. He would have to put more study into that. Often, the way John pronounced some of the words became clues, but he had no reference as to where those pronunciations were common. The most obvious one was his manner of agreeing with you. Most people just say, "Yes." John always answered, "Yeah." He also clipped his words. Most people draw out their words and in some cases almost run them together, making them easy to understand. That is usually referred to as a drawl. John cut his words clearly, pronouncing each.

After the sheriff visited John several weeks earlier, he had left a note for the doctor with Molly at the switchboard. That note assured the doctor that the sheriff no longer considered John to be a dangerous person on the run. It also noted that the sheriff might be able to find a proper name for John in a few weeks. This good news had been changed after the sheriff's last visit. The new good news was that the sheriff was still looking for missing person reports, although none of them fit John's description.

The age question was still on the doctor's mind. He really didn't need to know for any major medical reason other than if it would have a bearing on his amnesia. He was just curious. He had examined John and, from everything he could equate from his years of practice, John had the muscles of a young man in his early twenties. His skin was not wrinkled and his hair was still blond, with no signs of gray. His blood pressure was in the normal range for a man in his twenties and he could find no signs of age-related diseases that would be associated with a man much older. From this, he decided age could not have been a contributing factor to the amnesia.

But what had caused the amnesia? In going over the records, he found no physical reasons that John should have lost his memory. Summarizing his observations, he made a few notes. *There are no signs of trauma on his head and he doesn't seem to have headaches that would be associated with a head injury. He seems to be able to remember things from day to day and is progressing with the crossword puzzles. He can hold a conversation on those things he knows, but does not find the personal side of the memory the rest of the population depends on for their base. The only possibility left is that some traumatic event has taken place that his mind isn't able to handle and this has blocked his personal memories. The memory of this event must have been blocked by his experience during or after the accident. The question is how to get past the blockage.*

CHAPTER 7

Thanksgiving Day came and things slowed down at Williamson Memorial Hospital. There were no elective surgeries; for some reason, no woman was threatening to deliver her baby; and any problem that could be put off was. The only patients who were not able to go home were those still running a fever or confined because of some injury. The several that had relatives were expecting a lot of company and even a nice Thanksgiving dinner.

The doctor was home with his family eating a fine turkey with dressing and pumpkin pie. The sheriff was likewise home with his family enjoying his grandchildren.

John Rockhouse was still alone in his room with his door half closed so, according to the nurse, "he wouldn't be bothered by the noise in the hall." His only visitors were the nurses caring for him. His only company was the book of crossword puzzles he was working on. The loneliness had been building in him over the last few weeks. If he knew where home was, he supposed that this would be what homesickness would feel like.

The hospital routine continued. He had hoped that it might change for Thanksgiving Day, but other than the hospital being essentially empty, nothing had changed. Breakfast this morning was served early, as usual, and again it was bland, but he was promised a great Thanksgiving dinner.

He had to admit, the dinner was pretty good. On his plate, he found turkey breast, mashed potatoes, cranberry sauce, and a bun. There was even pumpkin pie for desert, although it was a very small slice. He took his time eating. Actually, he was killing time eating! It was going to be a long afternoon.

When the shift change happened, he was pleasantly surprised to see Nurse Radke. She was not her happy, pleasant self, though. She was professional, she was efficient, but her usual glow was not there.

Actually, Nurse Radke, Miss Susan Anne Radke, was homesick. This was the first Thanksgiving away from family. Even when she was in Milwaukee at school, Milton was close enough so some of her family could spend a little time with her on the holidays she worked. On the holidays she had off, she would go home to the farm. She had called them on the phone at noon and had said hello to everyone there, but when she hung up the phone she felt more alone than before she called. She was definitely feeling homesick!

She had been in Williamson since September. She had passed the state nursing license exam and she had settled in at the boarding house she called home, but she had not found any close friends. Had she gone to a large city, she would have found a Missouri Synod Lutheran Church and, by now, would have made some local contacts. As it was, the closest Lutheran church she had located was in Charleston, ninety miles away. To get there, she would have to take a bus, as she was in no position yet to buy a car.

She thought back to her home on the farm outside of Milton. Her grandparents were there. Grandpa Radke, a Goldwater backer, would be arguing politics with Grandpa Schneider, who looked at Lyndon Johnson as the savior of the poor. They each had retired from their respective farms and bought retirement houses in town, but they each had survived the great depression and they carried their politics forward from that point of view.

The grandmas would be helping her mother in the kitchen and at three this afternoon, would be cleaning up the leftovers from a great noon meal. In another hour, her father and brother would be in the barn first feeding and then milking the cows while they listened to the end of the professional football game on a radio balanced on the beam at the center of the barn. Every year, one of the professional football teams would play the classic Thanksgiving Day game in Detroit. This year, it was the Green Bay Packers against the Detroit Lions in Detroit. Even if their Green Bay Packers weren't playing, they would be rooting for the team that would, by winning, give their Green Bay Packers the best chance to be in first place in the League.

And here she was, the low person on the totem pole, working on Thanksgiving Day while most of the nurses, due to the low hospital census, had it off. And what was she going to do anyway? She and the other nurse had only five patients between them and four of them would have company. She would chart, pass out meds, and try to chase the visitors out of the rooms at eight, not that they would leave right away.

This was her state of mind as she entered room number twelve to care for John Rockhouse. It was no wonder that John noticed her lack of spirit this afternoon. As she was making observations and writing on the chart, John decided to try to break the ice.

"So how have you been celebrating Thanksgiving Day today?" he asked.

She didn't answer. She just continued to fuss about in his room. *Well,* he thought, *something must be wrong, as she usually would have responded with some humorous remark.*

Silence followed and, finally, she left the room.

At supper time, she brought in his tray.

"Here is your supper such as it is," she said as she placed it on the bed table.

"Thank you," he said as he reached up to the trapeze and positioned himself in his bed so he could comfortably eat.

"It isn't much, but you won't starve," she answered as she turned to leave. "I'll be back to pick it up in a little bit."

John ate slowly, trying to kill time again with his meal. It was turkey, but while at noon he had breast meat, this time he was served some of the dark meat. There were mashed potatoes and green beans with a green jell-o dessert. Later, she came back and picked up his tray.

Later, John was working on his crossword puzzle when Nurse Radke entered the room.

"I just came in to see if you needed anything," she stated.

"Yeah, could you please adjust the cover over my leg, as there seems to be a draft that is causing it to feel cold," he answered.

"I can fix that." she said as she came around the edge of the bed and began rearranging the covers on his legs. She then did something he had never seen any of the nurses do. She sat down on the front edge of the cushion of the visitor's chair at the foot of his bed, but she seemed nervous and fidgety.

"Do you remember anything about Thanksgiving Day from where you came from?" she asked.

"I have a feeling that it was a big celebration. The turkey and pumpkin pie brought stirrings, but I have no details of what they are. What has your day been like?" he inquired.

"My day has been spent here caring for the few people not able to go home to celebrate with their families," she answered somewhat bitterly.

"At least you can go home tonight and be with your family then," he suggested.

"That would be nice, but my family is far away, actually. In Wisconsin," she answered. "I haven't seen them since I left to come here in September."

"That's too bad. I don't even know where my family is or even what kind of family I have," he replied. "Can you tell me something about yours?"

"They live on a farm, actually. Quite a large farm, really. It is about three hundred and forty acres," she mused.

"I think I know something about farming," John answered excitedly. "I think I have memories somewhere about a farm."

"We have cows on the farm. We milk fifty-six cows most of the time. Now it is just my dad and brother doing the milking, but before I went to school to be a nurse, I had my special barn chores every morning and every night."

"What kind of milking machines do they use?" John asked.

"Why, Surge," answered Nurse Radke.

"I remember something about De Laval milking machines."

"What kind of cows do you remember?"

"Guernseys, I think.

"We have Holsteins. My Grandpa Schneider had Jerseys and always called the Holsteins *hay burners* because, although they give a lot of milk, the butterfat content is much lower than the Jerseys, and you get paid on butterfat, not volume.

"Listen to you," laughed John. "You sound more like a farmer than a nurse."

"Well, I was a farmer's daughter longer than a nurse, so what do you expect?" she said laughingly.

"Why'd you come to work here in Williamson?"

She looked away toward the window and didn't answer for a long time. Finally, she said, "I wanted to go somewhere different to work. Try something on my own. Start an adventure. Meet exciting people. I never expected that I would become so lonely."

"Yeah, I know how you feel. I am pretty homesick myself, but I don't even know what I am homesick for. I have some vague feelings and maybe glimpses in the back of my mind, but I can't remember. The doctor seems to think I will eventually be able to break through and remember. That is why I keep working on the crossword puzzles. Maybe given more time I can break through and remember."

You told me a little about a farm, which must have come from your memory, which is a start," Nurse Radke reasoned.

"You can always call your folks after work tonight and talk to them. That might cheer you up," John suggested.

"I actually called them this afternoon before I came in to work. It didn't help. I think it just increased my desire to be there," she confessed. "Anyway, I feel better having talked to you tonight."

"I appreciate you coming in and talking to me. The nights get so long. Tonight has been a great help."

"I really must get down the hall and make sure none of the other patients need something." She got up from the chair and left the room.

When she came back later with the evening meds, she was her usual, professional self and it was as if their earlier conversation had never happened.

John laid back and replayed that short conversation back and forth in his mind. He learned several things from it. He remembered things, not many details, but things that had to be from his past. He would have a lot to tell the doctor when he saw him tomorrow afternoon.

Friday, the doctor made it to room twelve shortly after two in the afternoon. He and the nurse walked into the room while John was dozing.

"Good afternoon," he announced with a booming voice.

A startled John Rockhouse would have almost jumped out of bed if he hadn't been trussed up in the traction device.

"I see you are a little spirited this afternoon," said the doctor. "Did you have a good Thanksgiving?"

"It was a pretty empty day with not much happening around here. Yesterday evening, though, Nurse Radke and I were talking about Thanksgiving and her experiences back on the farm where she grew up. I know things about farming!" he said excitedly. "I know about cows and milking machines and I have been thinking about tractors! I think my memory may be coming back."

"That is good news. It is an improvement, for sure. Tell me about how this happened," the doctor asked in an inquisitive voice.

"Nurse Radke was talking about growing up on a farm and she talked about milking cows, Holsteins and Jerseys, and I remembered Guernseys. I had first asked about milking machines. I remembered working with a De Laval milking machine and they used Surge machines. I remember the difference between the two and why we used De Laval.

"We just have to find more things that you know about and build from there. There may be more words in the crossword puzzles that will trigger more memories. When you come to any of them, write them down. Make a list. We can then explore what about the words bring back memories," the doctor explained. "This way, we can work together to find your past."

"Yeah, I will do that," John said.

The doctor handed the chart to the nurse and turned to leave.

When will I get out of this traction anyway?" John called after him as he was walking through the door.

"In about two weeks, we will take a set of X-rays of the bone in your leg and see if it has healed to the point that we can place the cast on your leg," the doctor called back from the doorway.

"What happens after that?" queried John.

"When that happens, you will be free to leave the hospital," the doctor said. "You should be able to celebrate Christmas wherever you want."

"That brings up another problem, then. Where will I go? I have no one here and I don't know where I could go."

The doctor turned and stepped back into the room. "That is something we will have to work out."

"Another question I have that no one has brought up, who is paying for all this?" John questioned.

"At this time, that question has not yet been decided. It will depend on how well you recover and what can be worked out. Don't worry about that now. We will talk about that when you are well enough to work." With that statement, the doctor turned and left the room to continue his rounds.

The doctor went home that night and, after supper and after spending a few moments with his family, read some more about treating amnesia.

CHAPTER 8

It was the night before Christmas, or actually Christmas Eve Day, and all through the Williamson Memorial Hospital, all the patients possible were being prepared to be discharged to spend Christmas at home, this even applied to John Rockhouse. He was finally being released! He finally had his cast in place.

John was looking forward to this day since December 14th, when he found out that the next day he would possibly have his leg placed in a cast. That didn't happen though. The doctor felt John needed two more weeks in traction before the bone would be good enough for the cast to be applied.

His leg was cast two days earlier and today he would get out of the hospital! John was ecstatic to get out of the hospital! He thought back about all that had happened in the previous two days.

There were problems on the day he was cast, the 22nd. He had been lying down for such a long time that when he first sat up, he was immediately lightheaded. It took him sitting up and standing for short periods to get his balance back. His cast was full length, starting at his hip and extending all the way down his leg to encase all of his foot except for the toes. Because they stuck out of the end of the cast, they had a tendency to get cold.

When he overcame his dizziness, he then faced the next challenge, the extra weight of the cast on his leg caused him to lose his balance. He had anticipated this and soon overcame that problem. The one thing he hadn't envisioned when he was originally told he would wear a cast was that his leg would be bent at the knee when the cast was applied. It made sense to him now, if his leg was not bent at the knee, he would not be able to walk with the crutches.

Now that he was up, there was the clothing issue. He realized he could not walk around the halls of the hospital on crutches with his tail sticking out the back of the hospital gown! When he asked about this, he was told that somehow the hospital had acquired enough donated clothing for him to have several changes of clothes to wear around the hospital and take with him when he was discharged.

Getting dressed was the next hurtle he had to overcome. Putting on shirts was an easy task. When it came to the underpants and the trousers, he had to learn a new skill. The boxer shorts would clear the cast and were easy. The one leg of the trousers went on real easy, it was getting the trousers over the cast where the challenge began. To make them fit, the outside seam of the cast leg was slit and ties were attached to each side of the slit. His challenge was to be able to tie the ties on the lower part of the leg. To do this, he had to bend his body in difficult ways to get his hands in position to make the bows.

Once he was walking with the crutches, he found he was weak. He had no endurance. When he was given the crutches and shown how to walk, he could only go a short distance before he had to stop to catch his breath. He had two days to build up his strength, but he worked at it and did it! The nurses also taught him how to negotiate stairs. He wanted to be ready to *get out*!

He was beginning a new phase in his life! He was on crutches, which gave him his first chance to explore what little of Williamson he could see from the hospital windows. While he was lying in bed, he was able to look through the window in his room and see the side of a mountain in the distance. During his trips to X-Ray he saw glimpses of rooftops, but not much else. Now he was able to go to various windows and doors to get a bird's eye view of the city. He crutched his way to a door to look out on the city.

The hospital was located halfway up the side of the mountain on what was almost a cliff looking on one side at the river valley and another side at the ravine that led down the mountain to the river. As he stood in a doorway looking out over the city, he began to make a mental map of what he saw.

To his left was the Tug River, winding its way through the valley. On this side of the river was West Virginia. Kentucky was across the river, accessed by three bridges. The land was flat for a ways on both sides of the river. The railroad track delineated the point where the flat land ended and the terrain began to rise and the top of the mountain began. The railroad track seemed to be about four city blocks from the river. On the flat side of the tracks, he could make out numerous multi-storied brick buildings, which he assumed were stores and city buildings. Up from the tracks began the rows of houses.

When he turned to look straight ahead, he looked across the wide ravine that continued to his right, up the side of the mountain. Perched precariously along the sides of the ravine was street after street of houses packed tightly together.

As he looked to his right, he saw the ravine and the houses come to an end to be replaced by the forest that made its way up to the peak of the mountain. On this cloudy, dreary, day in December, he looked over his new home in anticipation of what he was going to find there. As he looked, he tried to imagine the house in which he was going to live.

A couple of weeks before, the sheriff made an unannounced visit to John to discuss where he would go once he was released from the hospital. The sheriff knocked on the door of room twelve and said, "Hello, John. How are you doing today? I hear you are to be released from the hospital soon."

"I hope it will be soon."

"Where will you go when you are released?"

"I don't know," John answered apprehensively. I don't know what I am going to do, but I have to find someplace. I can't stay around here.

"We really don't have anyplace in the county system to put you until your cast is off. Yours is such an unusual case. You are in the crack between the different parts of the system. It ends up being my responsibility to house you. I can either house you in the jail, or I can farm you out. It will be cheaper in the long run for the county to farm you out. I have made arrangements for you to board with a family I know from church. They are older and all of their children have left the nest. They are the Wheeler family, George and Elizabeth. It will cost the county $22.50 per week for your room and board. I will expect you to repay the county when you are out of the cast and find work. Is that agreeable to you?"

"Yeah, that is very agreeable. Thank you. I will do my best to honor the trust you have in me."

"Then it is settled. Well, I must be getting back to work," the sheriff said as he turned and left the room.

John felt a wave of relief sweep over him. He now had a place to go. Where he would go concerned him, but he always felt something would happen to give him some place to go. Now he had the comfort of a plan.

He would be living with the Wheeler family.

In the evening, a day or two later, the Wheelers came to visit him in his room. They wanted to meet him and get to know him before they would be picking him up and taking him to their home. John had also wondered about them and was happy to meet them so soon. They walked in and George introduced himself, then turned and introduced his wife, Beth.

George Wheeler was a tall, stocky man with a wild crop of white hair which hung precariously down the front of his forehead, threatening to cover his eyes. He had the habit of continually trying to push it up higher, but it just wouldn't stay. His face looked weathered and his hands looked gnarled and worn, but his bright blue eyes showed a youthful vigor belying his age.

Elizabeth, better known as Beth, was tall for a woman, almost six feet by his reckoning. Her hair had only streaks of gray, her face showed few wrinkles, her blue-green eyes projected wisdom, and her whole appearance was that of a comforting loving mother. He felt an immediate attraction to her although he couldn't understand why.

The Wheelers lived near the hospital on the side of the ravine, up a block from the railroad tracks, east of downtown. They were both in their early fifties and their three children had grown and moved away. They attended the same Baptist church as the sheriff and when he made the appeal several Sundays back, they responded. Beth had told the sheriff, "This should bring some life back in the old house. It has been pretty dull around there since Duane, their youngest son, moved away."

George worked for the Norfolk Western Railroad since he graduated from high school and now was a yard man and no longer had to travel. He had thirty-five years of seniority and could usually work the hours for which he bid.

Beth, never worked outside the home and spent her life devoted to bringing up *her boys* and keeping a well-run home for her husband. Now that Duane had left home, she had been trying to find things to do to take up her extra time. Welcoming John into her home would fill that void.

The Wheelers made it a point to visit John several times before he would be discharged.

Back in his room after his walk, he sat in one of the guest chairs to rest. He thought about some of the things he was going to miss when he left the hospital. He would miss the structure brought about by the routine of hospital life, he would miss the help the nurses gave him as he fought over filling in the spaces of the crossword puzzles, and he would miss all the help Nurse Radke was giving him in his search for his memory. It was with her help that John cataloged personal things about his past.

He determined he was a religious person. He said a prayer every night before he went to sleep, he remembered prayers from his youth, and although he could not bring back complete memories, he could remember bits and pieces of his religious faith.

It was during a conversation with Nurse Radke that the subject of celebrating Christmas came up. She had been telling him how exciting it was to see how the people of Williamson were celebrating Christmas. She compared this to how her family celebrated Christmas on the farm. She told him about her planned trip to Charleston. She had three days off and was going to take the bus to Charleston to go to church on Christmas Day. He had a vague memory of Christmas trees, presents, the birth of Jesus, and the inside of a great church. His problem was putting this all together to mean something.

One day, while she was in his room taking care of something, she began asking him about what he could remember about Christmas. He mentioned a tree and some presents. She asked him what religion he was. This got him to thinking and the result was that he knew, but couldn't remember! He began asking some of the other nurses about religion and found they mentioned Catholic, Baptist, and Methodist. When he asked Nurse Radke which of these churches she went to, she told him that she was Lutheran and the easiest church for her to attend was Redeemer Lutheran Church in Charleston.

About the time his X-ray was taken, he began to hear Christmas carols from the radio he could occasionally hear from down the hall. Then, one evening, Nurse Radke came into the room humming one of the carols he had been hearing from down the hall, a tune that suddenly brought words from out of his memory, words that were different, but words he remembered learning and hearing all his life. He began to sing along with her humming:

Stille Nacht, Heilige Nacht!
Alles Schlaeft, Einsam Wacht
Nur das traute, hochheilige Paar.

After the first three lines, she stopped humming. His singing in German totally surprised her. When she looked over at him, she saw him lying in bed with tears in his eyes, still mouthing the words to the song.

"What did you just sing?" she asked incredulously.

John looked at her, teary eyed, and stopped singing. "It just happened! It's something I remember. I learned it sometime, I guess."

"Do you know what it means?"

"I think it was sung in my church at Christmas time," he said tentatively. "I think it means silent night, holy night. I think it is German."

"Can we do it again?" she asked as she began to hum the tune again. She was familiar with the German version, as she had grown up singing it in her home church.

Together, they sang two verses in German before she completed what she had left to do and left the room.

In the days following, Nurse Radke and John explored more and more of the memories he had of his worshiping in church. He knew the same church service liturgy she grew up singing in her church. She tested his memory by singing with him responses such as the Kyrie, the Gloria in Excelsis, and the Triple Hallelujah. She would make it a point to hum one of those tunes when she came into the room to take care of him and together they would sing the response.

He was concluding that, indeed, he must be a Lutheran of German descent. Even though the doctor wasn't impressed by these memories, in his own mind, these were great steps forward in his quest to find out who he was.

As he continued to rest from his exercise, he had to admit more memories were coming back little by little. Although the doctor was helpful in getting him to decipher the meanings behind the words John had been writing, even though he and the doctor spent a lot of time on the list, John felt the most help was coming from his talking with Nurse Radke.

During this time, the doctor had pursued John's memories of farming and tried to determine the region he was from by talking about the farm crops that were grown, the animals found on the farm, and the seasonal weather patterns John could remember. They continued discussing the crossword puzzles. The doctor spent time at home at night studying the notes taken in these discussions with John about the words from the crossword puzzles.

He had narrowed the language pattern down to the upper Midwest. The pattern had to be from Wisconsin, Illinois, or Minnesota. During the course of the last month, he had come in contact with the new nurse, Nurse Radke from Wisconsin, who had a similar way of speaking. This, along with the studying he had done, led him to place John probably in Wisconsin. This became the first part of the profile he was compiling.

When he talked to John about the crops raised on the farm, he ran into some difficulty. John talked about raising corn to be cut for silage for the cattle and for ear corn to be shelled for grist to feed them. They discussed the growing season and John had commented that the new hundred to a hundred and ten day corn gave the best ears for feed. The normal one hundred and twenty day corn was used for silage. The doctor found that growing season would fit the southern part of Wisconsin. The oats, rye, and soybeans would also fit a greater region and be compatible with Wisconsin. When John talked about the tobacco crop, though, that really threw the doctor off track. *Tobacco is a southern crop*, he thought. *It is grown in Georgia, Virginia, Tennessee, and Kentucky.* That was a mystery still to be solved.

The animals John remembered could place him almost anywhere in the Midwest. The cattle were primarily milk cows, very few beef cattle. They were pastured in the summer and housed in barns in the winter. This was almost universal and not that helpful in pinpointing a region. The same could be said for the pigs, chickens, and ducks. The animals just were not much help.

The seasonal weather patterns again placed John in the upper tier of states. The cool, short summers, except for several hot weeks in the middle of summer and the long, cold, cloudy winters with a short fall and spring separating them would also fit for the upper tier of states. These would be found in Wisconsin.

The list of words also brought to light an interesting anomaly. This concerned sand and the making of glass. Where this fit the puzzle was unknown and there were really no ways to find the connection, no matter how hard the doctor tried.

John also told the doctor about his remembering some things about God and his prayers. As the time progressed, John told the doctor about his memories about church he had found with the help of Nurse Radke. He even sang the Christmas song *Silent Night* to him in German, not that the doctor knew if the words were correct or not. The memories from John's church life were interesting to the doctor and furthered his belief that John was from the upper Midwest. He encouraged him to think about those things also, but in his own mind dismissed them as not being relevant to finding where John came from or remembering his name, these were things that could be found almost everywhere.

In all of this delving into John's memory, the doctor had produced an in-depth profile on John, but this produced nothing detailed about his name or home.

John got up from the chair to practice more walking with his crutches.

The day he was going home, he walked to the hospital business office to discuss the financial aspects of his discharge from the hospital. He was made aware of the fact that he had run up a sizable bill during his convalescence. He owed the hospital over two thousand dollars. He was going to have to take care of that somehow. The office told him that, as soon as he was able, he would be offered a job as a janitor in the hospital. Once he was working, he could begin to pay back what he owed. There was as if, though, that gave a little light to the end of the tunnel. If John remembered his name and was an insured driver, his automobile insurance might cover most of the bill, in the mean time though, John would have to sign an agreement to pay the hospital the money owed.

John left the office and headed back to room twelve to await the doctor's last visit to sign his release forms. When he got there, he found George and Beth sitting in the two chairs waiting his return.

"Hi," he greeted them.

"Are they ready to let you go?" George asked.

"The doctor still has to sign my release," answered John as he lay down on the bed, exhausted from the short distance he had traversed on the crutches.

"We have the car outside on the drive, thinking you could come right out. George, do you think we have to move it?" Beth asked.

"Nah, it should be all right parked there," he answered. "I just hope the doctor gets here soon, though."

They waited for a few more minutes before the doctor walked in, followed by a nurse with a wheelchair.

John sat up and positioned himself on the edge of the bed, facing the doctor.

"How are you handling that cast, John?" he asked.

"Good, I think," answered John, not quite knowing what the doctor meant by the question.

"Are you still feeling dizzy when you get up?" the doctor queried.

"No, but I still get real tired when I go any distance with my crutches," John answered.

"I have signed your release papers and the nurse here will wheel you out to the car. I want to see you in my office in two weeks to see how you're getting along," the doctor said as he turned and left the room.

The nurse came over to the bed and helped John put on his leather motorcycle jacket so he wouldn't freeze in the cold weather between the hospital and the car. Then she helped him sit in the wheelchair and adjusted the leg support to hold his cast. She then turned the wheelchair toward the door and led the parade down the hall and out to the car. It was a late model, four-door Ford.

To accommodate the cast, John sat sideways on the back seat for the ride the couple of blocks to the Wheeler's home. As he looked out the window of the car, he pictured the map of the town he had in his mind and was more amazed at how the houses clung to the side of the mountain. His spirits were buoyed up by seeing the sun as it was setting into the mountains to the west. The weather was brisk with the temperature in the high 20s with a slight breeze and a cloudless winter sky. *He* felt liberated! Here he was, out of the hospital and out of the confines of the room he had been in for the last eight weeks. *He* was so happy to be out. His only regret was that he had not had an opportunity to say good-bye to Nurse Radke. *He* felt she had helped him remember so much and he was going to miss her ebullient smile and cheery words. *He* guessed she was on her way to Charleston to attend Christmas Eve and Christmas Day services.

"The Christmas tree is up and we decorated the house for your homecoming," Beth said excitedly.

"Now, Mother," George interrupted, "you know you did it for the boys too."

"Well, they won't be there until sometime after noon tomorrow and I want John to have a nice Christmas Eve with just us at home," she countered.

"I really appreciate you doing this for me," John interjected.

"It's something we can do for someone who is so far from home," Beth replied.

"Here we are," announced George as he pulled the car into a driveway. "This is where you are going to live."

The car pulled up to the driveway and they all got out. George helped him with his crutches as he made his way up the side steps into the house. Yes, the tree and the trimmings were gorgeous.

CHAPTER 9

Monday, July 12th found John back at the hospital in room twelve. No, his leg was fine. He was there for his first day of work. He reported to the housekeeping department and was introduced to his new boss, Mrs. Hain. His job would be to join the "dust patrol." This meant that when a patient's room was empty, he would do all the cleaning necessary to make it ready for the next patient. He was cleaning the very room where he had spent so much time! John had come a long way since his release from the hospital on Christmas Eve. As he stood there, mop handle in hand, he remembered what had happened to him since he left.

Christmas Eve had been a time of discovery. When he climbed the back stairs and entered the kitchen at the Wheeler's, it was as though he had entered a new world. He had gone from a white, sterile hospital room to a warm, friendly home.

The Wheelers house was not new. It was probably built in the late twenties. It was a two-story frame house with white painted clapboard siding on the outside. It had a sizable front porch. Inside, on the first floor were the kitchen, pantry, bathroom, dining room, living room, master bedroom, and front hall. The stairway to the second floor was in the front hall. The stairway to the basement was near the back door in the kitchen. Located on the second floor were three bedrooms, a bathroom, a sitting area in the hall at the top of the stairs, and a storage room. John would be living in one of the upstairs bedrooms.

The first thing John did in his new home was to climb the stairs and, with George's help, move into his new room. The room had a full-sized bed, a clothes dresser, a study desk with its own lamp, and a clothes closet. The walls were painted a light shade of yellow. There was a window looking out over the street on the wall near the desk. There were pictures of Pittsburgh Pirate baseball players on two of the walls and a mirror on the third. The colorful patchwork quilt on the bed had been handmade by Mrs. Wheeler. All in all, the room exuded a very homey atmosphere. John's life with the Wheelers was going to be very comfortable.

For the first time since the accident, John spent an evening without feeling lonely. It was Christmas Eve and he was out of the cold, white, sterile hospital room. He was with people who were trying to make him feel at home. The six-foot-tall Balsam Christmas tree was laden with aluminum tinsel and many colored, blown glass ornaments. The red, blue, and green Christmas lights were strung around the tree and shown through the tinsel in such a way as to make the tinsel glimmer.

Christmas Eve with the Wheelers had been very enjoyable, as they did everything they could to make him feel at home. The Christmas Eve meal was simply fried hamburger with mashed potatoes and gravy and green beans, but it tasted so much better than the hospital food John had become used to.

On Christmas Day, he met the Wheeler boys and their families. John watched with George and Beth as the grandchildren opened the presents laid out for them under the tree. While the children played with their new toys and the women retreated to the kitchen to prepare the Christmas feast, the men gathered around the TV to watch whatever sports shows were on. During the afternoon, John spent some time talking with each of the three brothers. He found out that he was now living in the room Duane lived in before he got married and left home.

Welcoming in the New Year was another time of celebration at the Wheeler home. Whereas Christmas had been a time of joy and reflection, New Year's was a time of celebration and promise. For John, it was a definitive time of hope and promise. He still had this great hole in his past that he kept trying to fill. The more reading he did, the more bits and pieces of the things he knew from the past came floating up out of that empty hole. He was making progress crutching around the house and soon would be crutching around out doors. George and Beth had been so much help. He felt they were treating him just like a son.

New Year's Eve was spent in front of the TV watching as the commentators remembered the highlights of 1964. During the evening, John helped Beth make preparations for the grand New Year's Day evening meal. Again, she would enjoy the company of her sons, daughters in law, and her grandchildren. The big event was watching as the ball was dropped at Time Square in New York City, welcoming in the New Year. George had to work that night, but Beth and John toasted in the New Year with a healthy glass of water.

New Year's Day brought moderately cold temperatures with gray skies. There was a hint of snow in the air, but nothing of consequence happened. George came home from work early in the morning and went right to bed. He wanted to be rested for when the grandchildren arrived. John was looking forward to being with his newfound "brothers."

The big event of the day, of course, was the Rose Bowl football game on TV. Everybody in the Wheeler family followed the West Virginia Mountaineers. The Mountaineers were in the Big East Conference and all their play had been decided. The Rose Bowl was between the winner of the Big Ten Conference and the winner of the West Coast Conference. This game was a tradition on the TV for many years now and this year it was between the Wolverines of Michigan and Oregon State. Although the Wheelers didn't have a dog in this hunt, the Rose Bowl game was always exciting to watch and the Wheeler men always enjoyed watching a good football game. The game ended with the Wolverines winning thirty-four to seven.

When John finally hit his bed that night, he gave a prayer of thanksgiving for this wonderful family who had opened their doors to him.

Now that he had a more normal life, John began to build his strength for the time when his cast would come off. On the days the weather was good, he would take his crutches and go out to walk as far as his strength would permit. He began by walking on the flatter streets so he wouldn't have to negotiate going up and down the mountainside. He would walk in one direction, rest a little, and drag himself back. He started by just making it to the end of the block. Day by day, he added more distance to his walk. Sometimes it was just a hundred feet, but day by day, he gained the strength he had lost during the eight weeks he had been lying in traction.

One of his biggest problems was keeping his foot warm. Two and three pairs of wool socks helped, but if it was still too breezy, they let in a lot of cold air. Sometimes he had to cut his walk short because his toes were too cold. He continued to make progress though. By Easter, he was regularly crossing the railroad tracks and walking downtown. He was now on speaking terms with many of the people he regularly met during his walks.

John spent the days when the weather was rainy or too cold for him to venture out reading in his room. During the first few weeks, Beth would go to Central Library and check out books for him to read. Later on, he would cross the tracks and walk through downtown to the library. He loved to spend time there reading books about the history of the area, current magazines, and the Williamson Daily News.

Easter Sunday fell on April 18th. By this time, he had gained enough endurance to walk anywhere he wanted to go. The days were warmer and he was spending more and more time away from the house. He had favorite places in Williamson to go. George would come home and talk about his work at the train yard, which piqued John's interest in the railroad. Many days, he would walk down East 4th Avenue to his favorite spot near Goodman Avenue to sit for hours watching the rail cars being shuffled together to make up a train. At other times, when he just wanted peace and quiet, he would walk down Prichard Street to what was called "the Old Free Bridge," where he could sit on the river bank and watch the Tug River flow by.

The Wheelers attended East Williamson Baptist Church. He was invited to join them in worship on Sunday and Wednesday nights. George had to work on some weekends and on some Wednesday nights and on those occasions just he and Beth would go. John was religious, he knew about God, and he prayed quite often, but he really couldn't get himself excited about the church services. They did very little to bring back memories from his past. It was as if the whole service was foreign to him. John had faint gnawing feelings that Easter was in some way special for him, but try as he might, he could not remember why.

He became acquainted with some of the church members. He regularly saw the sheriff at Sunday worship. On many occasions, they stood around and talked after the service. They generally discussed John's progress in both his physical recovery and his remembering. John learned that from all the checking around the sheriff did he still could find nothing that was of any help in learning anything about John. He talked to John about the future. The sheriff asked John what he expected to do when the cast was off. John said he planned to work at the hospital to pay off the debts he owed. The sheriff asked if John had thought about leaving to try to find his identity.

John's answer to that was simply, "Where would I go?"

Early on a warm sunny day in February, the sheriff had given John a ride to the top of the mountain to see his car. The wreck had not been moved and, other than having been somewhat covered by leaves, was just as the sheriff had inspected it four months earlier. John looked at the wreck and wondered how he had managed to get out alive. The sheriff made the same observation. They drove the road up the mountain from Barnabus, but John was unable to remember anything about the night or the accident. During the drive, John and the sheriff had a long time together in the car to talk. They examined the progress John had been making to remember his past. He was finding things out about himself from when he read things. He knew about farming and some things about making glass. His arithmetic abilities had not been affected. His vocabulary was improving with his continued work on the crossword puzzles and he knew how to take care of himself. The blank hole was anything about his personal history.

The sheriff explained to him that he was going to owe Mingo County quite a sum of money for his room and board with the Wheelers. John agreed that as soon as he was employed, he would begin to repay that debt. He had been promised a job at the Williamson Memorial Hospital as soon as he could work. At this point though, he had no idea how much he would be making, but he promised he would begin paying his debt as soon as he could.

The sheriff brought up a very good point though. He could not work until he had a Social Security Card. The problem was that to get this he would need a birth date and a place of birth, neither of which were known.

Problems like this were not unknown in the Kentucky and West Virginia mountains and were usually solved in some creative way. The sheriff and John went to the County Court House and obtained a lost birth record for him. They listed him as an orphan born around 1940 in the mountains somewhere in Mingo or the adjoining counties. With this, they were able to get John Rockhouse a Social Security Card. Now, when he had healed, John would be able to go to work.

John's cast was removed after twenty-six weeks on Monday, June 28th at the doctor's office. This was a week before the July 4th celebration. The doctor gave him the okay to begin work on Monday, July 12th. This was so John could begin working the stiffness out of his leg before going to work.

After having his cast removed, his first order of business was finding new trousers. The ones he had were all slit down the side to make room for the cast. Now that the cast was gone, Beth took him shopping and she bought him gray work trousers that he would wear when he began working at the hospital. Somehow he felt as though she was treating him almost like a son. He felt at home with the Wheelers.

The Fourth of July celebration took place at the ballpark along Main Street across the rail road tracks on the riverside in Williamson. John likened it to a carnival. Since the Fourth fell on a Sunday, the day began with church, followed by the rest of the festivities.

The day took on a carnival atmosphere as one of the social events of the year sponsored by the Junior Women's Club coordinated by Mrs. Doyle Van Meter.

The festivities started with the one o'clock parade from the Williamson Field House to the West Williamson Softball Park. This was followed by a period of entertainment and a three-legged race. The beauty contest lasted from three thirty to four thirty, followed by another hour of gospel singing. By this time, everyone was hungry, so the picnic baskets were brought out. The swimming race was held from six to six thirty. By this time, everyone was ready for a break, many people sat around enjoying the lovely evening and those who wished went to Sunday evening church. The fireworks began at nine thirty. John's day finally ended with him upstairs in his bed trying to relax to go to sleep. His prayer that night was one thanking the Lord for his blessings.

On the day the cast came off, he hadn't realized how stiff and sore his muscles could be until he tried to take his first steps using the leg. That night, he lay in bed with muscle pain where he didn't even think he had muscles. He now knew why the doctor gave him the two weeks before letting him go back to work. It was to allow him to get these muscles back to where he could be up on them all day without having to rest all the time. He knew what he had to do. He had to stretch these complaining muscles out tonight and begin walking again for the next week. He turned over in bed, said his prayers, and tried to sleep.

The doctor had watched John as he stiffly walked around at the 4th of July celebration. He looked at him and wondered what more could he have done to help John remember. He had worked with John on each of his checkups during the last six months. John was doing all that could be expected of him to heal the leg. It was the amnesia that bothered the doctor. He had been unable to break through. John had described the empty well he looks in now and then, how he knows things but has no way of bringing up details. The doctor wondered what he could have done differently to bring back John's memory. That was the nagging question. What more could he do? At least John was able to work and go on with his life. The doctor was still going to have John visit him at least once a month to chart his progress. He had totaled up his time and, by that reckoning, John owed him about thirteen hundred dollars. He decided that, at least for the time being, he would not submit a bill. John was going to have enough to do just to pay off the hospital and the county right now.

CHAPTER 10

Thanksgiving finally arrived. John had been waiting for this day because he was to get his first holiday off from work and he *had plans*. If everything went well, this was going to be a wonderful day. So many things had happened to him now that he was working at the hospital.

He had started on Monday July 12, 1965. His first week back at work had been very tiring. He kept feeling pain in his leg, but he pushed himself and made his way through it without complaining. Mrs. Hain noticed that he was limping toward the end of the first day and questioned him about it, but he didn't want to complain and told her everything was fine.

He was excitedly looking forward to his first paycheck. He was paid the next week, Thursday the 22nd of July. This was when reality finally set in. He got his paycheck at the end of his shift, not from Mrs. Hain like the other workers. He had to go to the business office to get his. There, he was met by the business manager. The two of them talked about how he was to pay off the note he had signed when he was discharged from the hospital.

John had known that the bill he owed the hospital was exactly $2,016 because when he was released from the hospital, he signed a paper promising to pay this back as soon as he had a job. At that time, he had no idea of how much his payments would be since he had no idea what his income would be. Now that he knew, it was time to work up a payment plan.

The Mingo County Sheriff's Department had been paying his room and board. He had promised to pay the sheriff back as soon as he could. Now he was expected to figure out how much to pay the hospital every week. He didn't know how much he owed Mingo County. The doctor hadn't even mentioned a bill yet.

John sat in front of the business manager's institutional gray steel desk. The business manager asked John just how much money he needed a week to live.

This was when John realized just how tight things were going to be for him. Together, they worked out a budget. He was earning $1.25 an hour, working eight hours a day, six days a week, which gave him an income of sixty dollars a week. Of course, Federal Income and Social Security taxes were deducted and his take home was actually $50.78. It was from that number that they began to figure how he was to pay the hospital back.

His expenses were tallied up. They were listed as follows:

Room & Board	$ 22.50
Clothing	2.50
Incidentals	2.00
Food at work	3.00
Entertainment	1.00
	Total $ 31.00

This was what it would take for him to live. When that number was subtracted from his take home pay, his disposable income became $19.78 per week. The only question was how much of that would go to the hospital? John explained that he was going to have to pay back Mingo County for the recuperation time he spent at the Wheeler's. Together, they calculated that that would be around $630.00. They decided the hospital would take $15.20 a week, which would pay off the debt in a little over two and one half years. John signed a new note to the hospital stating those terms. That left $4.58 a week to pay the county. That would probably pay the county off in just over two and one half years also. The money for the hospital was to be withheld from his paycheck. He would receive a grand total of $35.58. Being as he had no time to make it to the bank that day, as a courtesy, the business manager cashed his check. He was given the $35.58 in cash and a receipt for the balance.

As part of his room and board, Mrs. Wheeler packed him a lunch to take to work each day. He really didn't need any spending money yet, so when he went home that night, he counted out $4.58 to give to the sheriff and gave Mrs. Wheeler the whole $31.00. He would still owe her a little for the new clothes she had bought him, but of all people he had to pay, it was the Wheelers he wanted to square with first.

On Sunday morning after church, John sought out the sheriff and explained his budget to him and what he had promised to pay the hospital each week. At this point, he gave the sheriff his pay envelope, which contained what was left of his first paycheck, the $4.58. The sheriff had a very surprised look on his face when he counted the money. He told John that he would give him a receipt for the money next Sunday. They talked and decided that an envelope on Sunday would be the easiest way to continue to pay off the debt.

John didn't have a social life to speak of. He went to church with the Wheelers and read books at the public library. Now that he was working and had been issued a new Social Security Card, he qualified as a resident and could check out books on his own. His extra time was either spent reading, sometimes at home or sometimes at the Central Library, though there were times when George invited him to watch televised sporting events with him. This really was not much of a problem though, as there were not many places John really wanted to go at night anyway.

Williamson was a small town, and the people were generally friendly, but somewhat clannish when it came to him. He talked differently than they and he felt he just didn't seem to fit in. When he was in his cast, he talked to the people he regularly met on the street during his walks, but the only people he could really call friends were the Wheelers. The sheriff was always very cordial to him, but deep inside he always felt the sheriff was never really certain that he was not a felon on the run. Because he really didn't have a pressing need for it, it was very easy to give his whole week's wages to Beth Wheeler to pay off some of what he owed.

At work, he didn't really make a lot of friends either. He was the only man in the housekeeping department. He cleaned the rooms and helped out in the laundry. The women were civil to him, but they had nothing in common with him. He heard them talking about their children, husbands, relatives, and dogs. None of these things interested him and he had nothing to add to any of their conversations. The people he could talk with were in the Engineering department. These were the men who maintained the facility. He understood the mechanics behind what they were doing and even how to wield the wrenches. They talked about hunting, fishing, hobbies, and sports. The only problem was that he seldom had an opportunity to talk to them. Their work was all over the hospital and they took breaks at different times from when the ladies took theirs.

The one person he did get a chance to talk to on occasion was Nurse Radke. Now that he was working at the hospital he called her by her given name, Susan.

Susan and John compared notes about how it was to live in Williamson. Susan had many of the same problems John faced. She worked three to eleven p.m. That was her shift and until she built up seniority and someone on first shift decided to retire or quit, that would remain her shift. She had no good way of meeting young people other than at church. The way it worked, she had been able make it to Charleston for Christmas Eve and Christmas Day and a few other Sundays after that. Her next big visit was at Easter. As she explained it to John, she had tried several of the local churches, but she was baptized *Lutheran*, grew up *Lutheran*, was confirmed *Lutheran*, and was not comfortable changing to anything else and that was that.

The way the schedules were written, she had only one weekend in three weeks off and it was almost impossible to make the round trip bus ride to Charleston every Sunday to make it to church and get back in time for work too.

Sometimes, she would come in early and the two of them would be able to meet toward the end of his shift. He always enjoyed talking to her. She teased him about being her older brother. He kidded her about bringing the farm with her into the hospital making it harder for him to thoroughly clean.

Susan boarded with an elderly lady just a few blocks from where John lived. As the fall wore on, John was able to come by and call for her on two of the Sundays she had off, she chose not to make the bus trip to Charleston for church on those two Sundays. The first time was in September. John hadn't bought a fall coat, so he was wearing his black leather motorcycle coat and work trousers when he rang the doorbell at the house where Susan lived. He was met at the door by her landlady, who looked him up and down disapprovingly before letting him in the door.

"Susan said she was expecting you."

"It is such a nice fall day, I thought we could go for a walk and enjoy the sites."

"Well, bring her back in time for dinner. Susan, he's here," yelled the landlady.

Susan entered the room from the kitchen. The sight of her almost took his breath away. This was the first time he had seen her out of her nurse's uniform. She looked so beautiful in the gold colored sweater and matching gold colored corduroy slacks. She carried a tan colored light fall jacket.

"Hi. You look beautiful today," John stammered, trying to give her a compliment.

"Thank you, John," she replied with an impish smile on her face.

"Let's go," John said as he stepped to the door, opened it, and motioned for her to precede him through it.

They left for a long walk.

Although John still had a slight limp, he had built up his stamina to the point that he had no trouble out walking anyone who would go with him. Susan, though, had no trouble at all keeping up with him. Walking was what she did every night she worked.

On this first Sunday afternoon they were together, John showed her around some of the favorite places he had found while he was crutching around Williamson. They walked to the downtown area and he showed her the library, the Coal House, the court house, and the spot on 4th Avenue where he would watch the railroad coal cars be assembled into coal trains. As they approached the steps leading up to the front door of the boarding house, a very nervous John was thinking, *How do I say goodbye to her? How do I tell her how much I enjoyed this afternoon without sounding stupid?*

"Well, we got you back in time so you won't miss dinner anyway."

"Yes, we certainly did," Susan responded.

"I hope you enjoyed your tour of Williamson," John said hoping the answer would be positive.

"I have been to downtown Williamson many times, but I had never thought of watching the coal trains being put together and I did enjoyed your company," she said laughingly.

"Let me see you to your door," John said as he took her by the hand and they went up the steps to the porch.

They arrived at the door and John, trying to be a gentleman, reached to open the storm door for her as she reached into her purse for her door keys.

"I really enjoyed walking with you this afternoon. Would you go walking with me again the next Sunday you have off?" John asked tentatively.

"Yes, John, I will be happy to go walking with you on the next Sunday I have off," Susan replied with that impish grin.

On the second Sunday afternoon they were together, the weather was cooler, so they spent some time in Central Library. John was always very careful about how long the walks took. He had to have her home by supper time or she would go hungry, as her landlady was very strict about when she served the evening meal. John would have really liked to take Susan out to a restaurant to eat, but on his budget, this just wasn't possible.

As Thanksgiving got closer, Susan talked to John about being home with her family for their yearly Thanksgiving celebration. John thought about how lonely he had been last Thanksgiving laying there in that bed and how she had cheered him up and opened some avenues of his memory. In light of this, he asked Mrs. Wheeler what it would cost to include Susan in their Thanksgiving festivities. Mrs. Wheeler thought that it was a good idea and she personally would invite her if that was what John wanted. John told her he had some ground work to lay but would get back with her.

A couple of days later, John and Susan were together in the break room and John brought up the subject.

"Do you have Thanksgiving Day off?" he asked.

"This year I do. I now get every other holiday off and since I worked on the 4th of July, I get Thanksgiving," she answered. "Why do you ask?"

"Well, I have it off also," John answered. "What are you going to do to celebrate?"

"I am pretty much on my own. My landlady will be out of town and I guess I will spend the day just catching up on things," Susan answered.

"Would you be open to an invitation?" John carefully asked.

"Depends on what kind," she answered with that impish grin on her face.

"For dinner at the Wheelers," he carefully answered and fearing she might say no added, "Mrs. Wheeler said she would call you and invite you in person if it is necessary."

"I don't think that will be necessary," Susan answered. "Tell her I will be there. What time is it?"

"The Wheelers usually do things in the afternoon, so I suspect everyone will start arriving sometime around two and we will eat around six. I would like to come over and call for you after noon and we can walk around a little before we get to the Wheeler's," John suggested. "I've been a little long on my break and must get to work. I'll tell Mrs. Wheeler to count on you, though."

John left and went back to wrapping up his shift work for the day.

Thanksgiving Day, John got up early and joined Mr. and Mrs. Wheeler for breakfast. Mr. Wheeler had the day off and decided he wanted to watch the Macy's Thanksgiving Day Parade on the TV. John was too excited to just sit around and wait for the time to pass when he would go to get Susan, so he was in the kitchen doing whatever he could to help. The turkey was in the oven and was roasting to perfection; it was a very large one and would take most of the day to cook. The pumpkin pies were sitting on the shelf in the cool entryway to the back door, waiting for the time the whipped cream would be applied. The potatoes were peeled and in the water waiting to be boiled. The canned vegetables were lined up, ready to be opened. The cranberries were in the fridge waiting to be served. He was able to help with the jell-o molds, but they were now cooling in the fridge also. There really wasn't much more that John could do in the kitchen to help.

Mrs. Wheeler served them sandwiches for lunch. When lunch was over, John put on his coat and headed out to walk to Susan's and bring her back. The sky was overcast with gray-blue mottled clouds hanging just above the mountain peaks. There was a slight breeze wafting up the valley. John pulled his coat tightly around his body and put his hands in his pockets. The one advantage of the leather motorcycle coat was that it kept the wind out. The disadvantage was that when the leather got cold and pressed against the body, it sucked out some of the body heat. He could tell in the first block this was going to be a cold walk today.

He rang the doorbell and waited on the porch for Susan to arrive at the door. She appeared to be dressed warmer than he and probably would not even feel the cold. Originally, he had planned to walk down to the river at the Old Free Bridge and watch the water with her for a while before going back to the Wheeler's, but that plan was being modified by the cold. He enjoyed the last two times they had gone for the walks and spent time together. They talked about so many interesting things. He was hoping for the same result this time, but he decided the weather wasn't going to lend itself to a long walk today.

As they walked, she told him about the phone call she made to the farm at noon. Everyone there was well and about to sit down at the table. They are now milking sixty-two cows, so today they must get an early start on the barn chores. She wished they could come and visit her, but they just can't get away from the cows. Farming is like that!

They arrived back at the Wheeler's earlier than he had planned, but Duane and his wife were early too and Susan was introduced to all who were there. Soon thereafter, the other two brothers with grandkids in tow arrived and the home became lit up with the chaotic sounds of a happy family. The men, engrossed in football, were in front of the TV in the living room cheering when a great tackle, run, or interception was made. The younger children, not in front of the TV, were playing games, squabbling among themselves, and generally chasing about interrupting the adults wherever they were. The women retreated to the kitchen, where they found some semblance of peace and quiet and sat around the kitchen table to talk. Susan had been invited to join them in the kitchen and did so for some time while she got to know them, but as the conversation continued into the discussion of the more personal family things women generally discuss, she thought, *I don't know these people, it's as though I am eves-dropping on the personal lives of total strangers,* and then she went to the living room to join John in front of the TV. Eventually, she noticed the women setting the table for the meal and thought, *I'm eating here and I want to do something. Maybe at least I can help to serve the meal,* and went to lend a hand.

The cheering finally died down in the living room and the grandchildren seemed more subdued in time for the Thanksgiving dinner to be served. The women placed the food on the table, the children were rounded up, and the men were called and everyone was seated. Mr. Wheeler blessed the food and everyone dug in to eat. When the meal was done, they all sat around the table and talked about what they were planning for the Christmas season.

Finally, Mrs. Wheeler got up to clear the dishes. Susan pitched in with the other women and helped her. While they were in the process, Mrs. Wheeler made a special point to try to make Susan feel at home.

"You must be very lonely here being so far away from your family," she said to Susan.

Susan looked up in surprise as she spoke and answered, "It has been hard being so far away. Working the second shift has been hard too, as I really have not been able to make a lot of friends in Williamson. The nurses I work with are older and have families and we have very little in common. It is very hard to meet people when you work when they have off. I took care of John sometimes when he was in the hospital. He is the only friend I really have and I don't see him all that often."

"Do you have a church home here in Williamson?" asked Mrs. Wheeler.

"I am Lutheran and the nearest Lutheran church is in Charleston. I have to take the bus to Charleston and the connections are not that good. I am off on the weekend every three weeks, so I don't make the trip very often. I do have several girlfriends up there, but we are so far away we don't do things together," she replied.

"I would like to invite you to come to church with us. There are a lot of younger people you could meet there," Mrs. Wheeler responded.

"It might be interesting," she answered while thinking, *I have already tried visiting other churches and I know how I feel.*

"You know, John comes to church with us on Sunday and Wednesday," Mrs. Wheeler explained. "It would be real easy to pick you up too."

"I have visited several local churches during the past year and not been drawn to any of them," she explained, trying to be courteous and yet not commit to anything.

"We can pick you up and take you, you know," Mrs. Wheeler continued.

"I do have Sunday mornings free, even the Sunday's I work," Susan blandly answered.

"We would really like to have you."

"I think I'll try it. I can let John know when," she answered not wanting to hurt Mrs. Wheeler's feelings by turning her down, but still knowing in her own mind that it probably would never happen.

"It was so nice that you could come and be with us today," Mrs. Wheeler said.

"Thank you so much for having me. I did feel like I was at home," Susan answered, being polite.

"Seeing as you have no family here, would you like to join us for the Christmas and New Year's meals we have? Just think of us as your home away from home," invited Mrs. Wheeler.

"I will have to see. That will depend on my work schedule," she answered, not wanting to say no, but not wanting to commit either.

Susan and John enjoyed the festivities for a little longer and then Susan thanked the Wheelers again for inviting her and asked John to walk her back home. On the way back, they began to talk about the afternoon.

"Did you enjoy the afternoon?" John asked, having noticed that she didn't seem like her usual self.

"It was nice. The Wheelers are a nice family," she answered. "Mrs. Wheeler and I talked a little bit."

"That was good. I thought you were feeling out of place."

"I did for a while and I think Mrs. Wheeler tried to welcome me into her family."

John was silent for a while as he thought about how to answer her. "I think I was invited into the family last Christmas when I was released from the hospital. They have treated me like a son."

"Do you still think you are Lutheran?" Susan asked.

"I really don't know," he answered.

"Mrs. Wheeler said you go to the Baptist church with them."

"I do, but it just doesn't seem right. I am not a Baptist. It just doesn't fit," John stated.

"Mrs. Wheeler asked me if I would go to church with them. I told her I am Lutheran and attend when I can in Charleston, but I would think about it," Susan responded.

"The people there are real friendly. You might enjoy going."

John began to think that *this would give him more time to get to know Susan.* He had found her fascinating the first day she had cared for him at the hospital and now he certainly enjoyed her company. His hope was that she enjoyed his enough to still spend time with him.

"I told her I would tell you when I wanted to go to church with them. You could then let them know," she concluded, thinking, *I'm still Lutheran, I don't have to join the church, and I will be able to get to know John better.*

"I can do that."

They continued to talk about things in general and finally they were at her landlady's door. She unlocked the door and had it slightly open when she turned to face him. From deep inside, John felt the urge to hug her and kiss her good night as though he had done this so often before. But from some other area inside him came the admonition to treat all women with respect, so he looked into her eyes, held both her hands in his, and wished her good night.

The night was cold, the clouds had cleared during the day, and the cold had caught up to John, so he hurriedly walked back to the comfort of the Wheeler's warm house.

That night, he said his prayers and went right to sleep. It truly had been a wonderful day.

CHAPTER 11

Valentine's Day found John Rockhouse in a jubilant mood. Things in his life were going along really well. Granted, as of yet he had not been able to remember his name or his past, but he was building on his current successes and on the things he was remembering from his work on the crossword puzzles. He had bought a great new dictionary, which was helping him to remember more and more things to add to his general knowledge.

He was still having his monthly visits to the doctor to try to delve into his past. These were very frustrating for both the doctor and him. He felt as though he had holes in his brain. They tried to work on some part of his background. The idea was to expand his memory of things he already remembered, such as his background in math. He did very well at solving math problems, but when it came to remembering how he learned his math there was a great void, a chasm with no bridge. He could name none of the teachers from whom he learned what he now remembered. At other times, the doctor would ask him a question and deep in his mind he knew that he knew the answer, but he could not remember it to answer the doctor. All in all though, he did feel he was making progress!

His work at the hospital was going well. He was now helping the Engineering group when they needed an extra hand. This came about after he heard one of the older men in the department was looking at retiring. John asked if he could be considered for a transfer to become the low man on that totem pole. The answer came; he would be considered. It looked as though they were trying him out at every opportunity. He liked those jobs a lot better than the housekeeping work he normally did. He didn't know what the pay scale would be, but he knew it would be a raise.

With George's encouragement, ever since Christmas, John had been looking outside the hospital for a job that would pay more money. He felt a great inner pressure to get his debts paid off. There were still two more years to go on both the hospital and the county debts and the doctor finally presented him with a bill. This was just another $750 to pay off.

John talked a lot with George about where he could go to improve this income. He asked about the prospects of working for Norfolk and Western Railroad. George took him down to the yard and helped him fill out a job application, but railroads in general were having hard times and tended to hire family members before outsiders, so nothing ever happened there. He looked into coal mining, but again he didn't have the background they were looking for. He talked to the sheriff about finding a place in his office, but the drawback there was obvious. He couldn't overcome the background check. There were a myriad of other jobs available that would pay him what he was making at the hospital and the working conditions would be worse. It came down to his bettering his pay through promotion at the hospital.

His life at the Wheeler's was comfortable. His room was very homey. It was a great place to read. Several months ago, he bought a used radio, which he listened to at night and on special occasions George would invite him to watch TV. At Christmas and New Year's he had again been treated as part of the family. Susan was again invited to join them and they celebrated New Year's Day together.

John was proud of the fact that he had been able to save a little money. He was frugal enough to have saved fifty-two dollars in the last seven months. Right after he got his W-2 forms from work, he filed his Income Tax and he was awaiting a tax refund of $84.80. He had no idea where he was going to spend this, as the list of things he could use was so long, but replacing some of his worn clothes was high on the list. He was okay with his work clothes, but it was his Sunday clothes that he wanted to update. An appropriate suit would be thirty-five dollars and a white shirt would run $1.95. He also had his eye on spending $2.50 for a necktie. Of course, if he got the suit, he would also need an overcoat to wear outside, and then gloves, and finally Oxford shoes. He had hopes of covering all of these things with the tax refund check.

Susan and John were spending a lot more time together. Even though she was Lutheran, she attended church with John and the Wheelers on many Sundays. She began joining them for church two Sundays before Christmas. She saw John at work and asked him if they could pick her up to come to church with them. John made all the arrangements and they picked her up on the way to church that first Sunday. The weather was mild that day, so after church she suggested that John get some exercise and walk her home. John took that as a good sign and the two took a leisurely walk to her home. They had a nice talk along the way. This became the habit they followed from then on. On the Sunday's she had off, the walk home after church turned into an invitation by her overly protective landlady for John to stay for lunch. On these days, when the weather was good, they would take a long afternoon walk either down to Goodman Avenue to watch trains or to the Tug River to stroll along the bank. John enjoyed her company and he had the feeling she enjoyed his.

After the first of the year, she began to talk to John about buying a car. She asked him what he thought of the idea. She explained that over the past seventeen months, she had saved a little over $1,800.

"What is the best kind of car to buy," asked Susan.

"I guess that depends on what you want the car to be like," answered John.

"That's not much of an answer. It doesn't tell me anything!" Susan shot back. I want you to tell me what kind of car you think I should have."

"Before I can answer that I need to ask you some questions, do you want a new car or an old car? How much do you want to pay and what make do you like?" John answered.

"I really don't know. I'd like to get a new car, but I don't want to spend all my money either, so I guess a used car might be the answer," she mused.

"What make do you like?' he continued. "I remember some things about Ford cars, and the one laying upside down up on Mystery Mountain is a Ford.

"Dad has always driven a Hudson, they are roomy and I like driving them. One grampa has always driven a Plymouth and the other has always driven Fords," she explained.

"I think what it boils down to is you need a good used car that is affordable and easily serviced here in Williamson," John concluded.

"Can you come with me while I look for a car?" she asked.

"We can go on the Saturday mornings when we are off work to see what we can find." suggested John.

Unfortunately John was not much help going with her to look at cars. He worked the day shift, she worked the evening shift and the only time they really had together to look for a car was on Sundays when none of the car dealerships were open.

One of the cold Sunday mornings in January, when John decided to accept George's offer to drive Susan and him to church, George made the offer to help Susan find a suitable car. This would work out rather well, as George usually had Saturday's off and even if she worked on Saturday she didn't have to be at work until 3:00.

The very next Saturday, George and Susan went out to look around for a used car. George was looking for a car in the $1,200 range that had good tires, low mileage, and was clean looking and very reliable. After all, George didn't want Susan's car to break down on the road somewhere. They saw several that the local dealer had on the lot, but George found something he didn't like with each one. That first Saturday ended with Susan feeling there wasn't a car in Williamson that fit the specifications George was insisting on. That Sunday was a bright and cheery, but cold day, and after church, Susan again asked John to walk her home. She wanted to talk to him about her car hunting on Saturday and how depressed she was over the cars they found. She appreciated George taking her under his wing and keeping her from buying something that she would have regretted, but she was afraid she would have to go to Charleston to find what she wanted. She told him of her dream of having a car that was so reliable she could drive it to Charleston on her Sunday off and go to church. John walked and listened, but there was really nothing he could say or do that would alter her situation. It was a Sunday and she worked, so he said good-bye to her at her door and left for his.

After lunch, she called her folks and spent a long time talking to her dad about the fact she wanted to buy a car. He recommended she find a make other than a Hudson as the Hudson Motor Car Company had merged with Nash, creating American Motors and who knew what would happen with that. Her father liked the idea that George was helping her pick a reliable car, but as far as recommending a specific make, he was no help.

Nothing much happened on the car hunting front for a couple of weeks, but on the evening of the third of February, George came home from work and told John he had news for Susan. He had found the car. The next day, when Susan came in to work, John should tell her she had an appointment Saturday at nine with George to go look at it.

Saturday morning, an excited Susan was over at the Wheelers by eight thirty, ready to go to look at the car.

"You are here early," commented George as she came in through the back door into the kitchen.

"I just didn't want to be late."

"We can't go see the car until after nine anyway, so maybe I should tell you a little bit about it. I have worked with this fellow for twenty-three years. He bought it new in 1954 from the Ford dealer in Charleston. It is a Ford Custom line standard two door. It is not fancy. It is two-tone blue; it has an economical six cylinder engine, a standard transmission, a radio, and new tires. He walked to work, so generally he only drove it on his days off. In twelve years, he has driven only 42,600 miles. The body shows very little rust and the paint is not faded. He is asking $550 for it and I think the car is worth it. Once you see it, I think you will like it," George explained.

"I'm ready to go when you are," Susan responded. "I really want to see this one. I have my check book and I have enough money. Can we pick it up today?"

"We might be able to, but we will have to see what he says. He may need it for a week or two yet," George answered. "Besides, you will have to get insurance and make a tag application, and did you ever switch over your driver's license?"

"I guess there is a lot more to buying the car than just handing over the money," she answered.

"Well, we had better be going. We don't want to be late!" George jokingly said.

Susan saw the car and immediately fell in love with it. She gave the man a check to hold the car and got the information from him she would need to get her insurance. He would need the car until the next Sunday and they made the arrangements to seal the deal on the 13th after church. Susan would be busy during the mornings several days next week, getting everything lined up so she could drive the car home the next Sunday after church.

Sunday, February 13th was a cold, dreary day, but the excitement of love was in the air. Monday was St. Valentines Day and, being it fell on a Monday, it was naturally being celebrated on Sunday! For weeks already, the 5&10 Cent stores had all the hearts and ribbons you would ever want to see and buy for the one you love. All the merchants had for sale stocks of everything you could imagine to appeal to a girl's heart. Several days after work, John had gone "shopping" for just the right card to give to Susan on Sunday. This was a difficult choice he had to make. John was attracted to her and had feelings for her, but he couldn't really define what those feelings were. They felt like the feelings he had been reading about in the books he checked out of the library, but deep inside there was this conflict. He couldn't get over the nagging feeling there was someone else, someplace, who had the rights to a piece of his heart. This nagging feeling bothered him to the point that he believed he must be very careful with his relationship with Susan. He cared for Susan and he did not want her hurt. The last thing he wanted was to have won her heart only to find out he had a wife and family someplace out there and have to leave her to keep his commitments.

He perceived that she liked him and she was definitely not seeing anyone else. Maybe he was just being paranoid. Maybe there was no one out there waiting for him. He just needed time to remember! That was it! Time to remember!

He finally made his choice for her Valentine's gift. He bought a two dollar heart-shaped box of chocolates and a thirty-five cent card to go with it. The card was to "My Very Special Friend," and had an appropriate verse inside. John signed it John Rockhouse, and then placed a question mark behind his name.

The Wheelers and John drove to Susan's house to pick her up for church. John brought his Valentine along just in case she would give him his Valentine when they picked her up for church. John went up to the door to call for her. She met him at the door and gave him his Valentine Card. He had to open it for her there. It was a very pretty card with hearts and flowers and the usual references to love. He opened it and read it. The only thing he could do after what it said was give her a great big hug. They then went to the car. George made some comments, his wife made the point of shushing him, and when they were settled in the back seat, John gave his valentine to Susan. By the time she had looked at the candies and read the card, they were parked at church. Any overt show of affection would have been inappropriate.

After church they got into the car and headed to pick up Susan's new car. All the papers were signed. The seller instructed Susan on how to run the car, where to check the oil, and how to keep the car looking good. Susan got in the driver's seat with John as passenger, said good-bye to all, and drove off.

Susan headed the car down toward the river.

"Where are you headed?" John enquired.

"I just want to go someplace. I have never really been out of town and I just want to see some of the countryside. I also want to get some heat in the car," Susan responded. She turned on the radio and started to tune in different stations. They began driving south toward the town of Matewan.

They just watched the scenery go by and listened to the radio. The novelty of it kept Susan busy just changing stations. There wasn't much on the radio Sunday around noon. As they passed through Matewan, the static got the best of her and she turned the radio off.

She looked over at John and said, "Thank you for that nice box of candy. The card was nice, but I don't understand how you signed it."

"Your card was very nice too," John replied.

"You still didn't explain how you signed my card."

"You know me as John Rockhouse. Everyone I know calls me John. Is that who I really am? The question mark is who am I because until I know my real name I will always have that question in my own mind."

"John, I like you a lot and I don't want that question mark to get in the way. Now that I have this car, will you come with me when I drive to Charleston to church?" she asked as she drove slowly along the road, looking for someplace to turn around.

"I will be happy to go to church in Charleston with you. Nothing would make me happier," John responded.

On Monday morning, St. Valentines Day, John played all of this through his mind as he walked up the hill toward the hospital. John was definitely in a jubilant mood.

CHAPTER 12

The July 4, 1965 fireworks were the best John had seen, which wasn't saying much since he only remembered them from last year, but that was the statement he made to George on the way back home afterwards. He had wished that Susan could have been there with them, but as almost always, she had to work. She had the previous Sunday off and they went to Charleston for church, but the fourth fell on a Monday and she was scheduled to work. He didn't have Monday off either, but he didn't work evenings, so he was able to celebrate.

Tuesday of the next week was the one year anniversary of his starting to work at the hospital. Over the last year things had been going very good for him there. On March 31st, the fellow in the Engineering department was given his retirement party. On Monday, April 4th, John officially began his workday as a member of the Engineering group. This was a new job, more pay, and now he worked a forty hour week.

John sat down and recalculated his budget. The Wheelers had been good to him this past year and he was appreciative. He hadn't minded when, at the end of February, they had raised his Room and Board two dollars per week. His budget had absorbed the extra expense. Now with his new job, his disposable income had increased to $32.56. He decided that the doctor should begin to be paid and he would work that out with him at his next scheduled appointment. In the meantime, John decided he would just save the extra.

His new job was much more stimulating than his work with housekeeping. Now he would go with another one of the men and together they would fix whatever it was that had decided not to work or had been broken. He was becoming used to the extra day off he was now getting. However, now he was on the same type of day rotation that Susan was on and he didn't always have Sunday's off to go to church with her. Occasionally, they were both off on a week day or one day during the weekend.

Now that Susan had her own car, the adventuresome spirit which brought her to Williamson in the first place began to come out of hiding and she began exploring the area. She visited the little towns in the immediate area, but the city with the biggest shopping district was the city of Logan over the mountain in Logan County. This was not a hard drive, but it was slow going driving up US 119 and she didn't necessarily like to do it alone. She usually waited for a day she and John had off together to do her exploring there.

She took the first trip to Redeemer Lutheran Church in Charleston alone the first Sunday she was off after she bought the car. She had enjoyed the service and was back fairly early. She found she could cover the ninety miles in about two and one-half hours. She decided if she started really early on Sunday morning she could drive the ninety miles to Charleston to attend the morning service and if she left right after the last hymn, she could be back in time to go to work at three, but if the weather was bad though, she might as well forget it. She made the trip on several more of the Sundays she worked, but the schedule was tight, so she decided to only go on Sundays she had off. When she didn't go to Charleston, she attended church with John and the Wheelers. The next Sunday she had off was in March and she went to Charleston alone. That week, when she saw John at work, she invited John to go with her on the next Sunday they both had off. John reminded her that he already told her he would go the day she bought the car. It was settled then. John would go with her.

John had become a permanent part of her life. She liked him, he was fun to be with, and they seemed to have so much in common. In the beginning, she had looked at him almost as a brother, but over the last six months, he was the person she wanted to spend time with. She began to look at him as her boyfriend. He was a challenge though. He seemed so timid. She wished that just once he would put his arms around her and give her a kiss. She had hoped for that the Sunday before Valentine's Day. She got a hug when she gave him the card, but that was all. The moment had passed. She had wanted to give him a hug and kiss when he gave her his Valentine heart, but with all the people around, that was not possible. The candy and card he gave were very thoughtful, but he just was a little slow. And yet, she so enjoyed his company and felt very safe when she was with him.

The next time they both had off was the Sunday after Easter. It was Sunday, April 17th, and she and John made the drive up US 119 to Charleston to go to church.

John had been looking forward to the trip to Charleston for some time. This would give him new scenery to look at, a new town to explore, and travel time in the car with Susan. Although his concern about his past coming back to haunt him made him hold back any real show of affection for her, he was beginning to have some very deep feelings. He actually was more excited about spending the day with her than going to church. As they began their drive to Charleston, he had no idea how momentous this day would be in his life. He was not prepared for this to be the first day he recognized and remembered the something major from his past.

Susan picked John up at about six o'clock for the drive to Charleston. Church started at ten thirty, but on bad days the drive could take three hours. It was a slow drive through all the little towns along the way and they had a long time to talk. They arrived at church about an hour early, which gave Susan time to introduce John to some of her friends. He listened as she talked with them about work and some of the other things that were happening in her life.

When they went into the worship area, several things hit John right away. There was an altar with a cross and candles on both sides of the cross. To his right was a pulpit and to his left was a lectern. Then he looked through the worn, cloth-covered, blue hymnal the usher handed him. All he could do was excitedly whisper to Susan, "I know this book!"

"This is the Lutheran hymnal." she whispered back.

"But I know this book," he whispered again as the music began and they started to sing a hymn he recognized from his childhood. It was not Communion Sunday. He knew the page-five service by heart and didn't even open the book to sing the responses. He now knew he was a Lutheran. He just wished he could remember more. This was the first time in a long time he was excited about a church service.

Although he had been excited about the church service, once they began the trip back to Williamson, John became unusually quiet. They stopped along the way for a light lunch and as soon as he got back in the car, he sat on the right hand side of the seat, very close to the door. He didn't look over at Susan often, but when he did it was only to glance in her direction.

"What is the matter?" asked Susan.

"I have to think," he answered. "I have some almost memories and am so confused. I just have to think these through."

"Can you share them with me? Maybe we can work them out together."

"I don't know if you really want to know what is going through my mind," he carefully replied.

"They can't be that bad," she said, raising her voice, trying to make a joke.

"It's all confused and I don't want to tell you something that is not true," John pleaded as he turned his head again toward the window.

They continued along the road with John staring out the right hand window and Susan fumbling with the radio knobs, trying to find a strong enough station to hear something, anything, to take her mind off what John might be thinking on the other side of the car. On the one hand, she wanted him to regain his memory; on the other, she feared it might change their relationship.

It was when they came to Logan and slowed down even more for the traffic John broke the silence.

"Forgive me, Susan, for being so moody, but I think my first name is Heinrich, Henry for short. I think I have a second name, Karl, but I can't find the last name. I remember a pastor standing with his hand on my head at my confirmation and speaking the words Heinrich Karl, but nothing follows."

Susan looked over at him, turned the radio off, and in a tentative voice, said, "So you are beginning to remember some things. This is good, isn't it?"

"It is if what I remember is real, but what if it isn't? What if this is just from a dream? There are other things I have a glimpse of too. They are so contradictory that I can't share them with you."

"They can't be that bad! After all, I am a *nurse*! And I am your friend and you can always count on me," she stated in her commanding *nurse* voice.

"I will be seeing the doctor in a couple of weeks and maybe he and I can make enough sense out of this so I can feel comfortable telling you. Nothing has changed between us. You are still my very best friend and I still want to spend time with you. I don't want anything to change," John replied.

The rest of the way to Williamson, they talked about the sermon and church and going out to eat a Sunday supper together. Neither knew a really good place to eat, but they would find one. First though, they went by and told her landlady and the Wheelers not to expect them for dinner.

As the weeks turned into months, they made plans for the summer. John and Susan continued spending as much time together as they could. One of their plans was for Susan to take some vacation time and visit her family in Wisconsin. She wanted to make sure John would be able to take vacation and make the trip with her, but she hadn't asked him yet to go with her.

John's next visit to the doctor was memorable, indeed. He had news to report, discuss, and digest. He sat in the waiting room with the other patients, waiting for the nurse to call him to a room. When he was situated in the room, the doctor came in.

"How have you been getting along? Have you been keeping up with your math and crossword puzzles?" the doctor asked.

"I have, but I don't think they are really helping anymore.

"But I still think you should keep them up."

"I think I made a breakthrough a couple of weeks ago," answered John excitedly.

"And what might that have been?" The doctor seemed skeptical.

"I went to church the Sunday after Easter," John answered.

"That's not new; you go every Sunday you have off with the Wheelers. Don't you? What made that Sunday so different?"

"I went to the Lutheran Church in Charleston! I am a Lutheran!" John responded.

"And what made you think that?" the skeptic within the doctor asked.

"I recognized the Lutheran hymnal and sang the Liturgical responses from memory!"

"What's so new about that? Weren't you able to do that with that nurse, what was her name, ah, Susan before you were released from the hospital?" the doctor asked.

By now, John was somewhat frustrated at the way the doctor was responding to his new breakthrough, so John answered excitedly, "I recognized the hymnal. The book, I knew what was in it! It's the first thing I have recognized, remembered, or been able to identify from the past!"

"That's not going to do us much good until you can remember your name and where you are from."

"This also opened up some other parts of my memory. I thought you would be interested in where that went," John remarked offhandedly.

In a kind of bored tone, the doctor said, "Well, tell me about it."

"It was after church on the ride home that I remembered something from my confirmation. It was my pastor—I don't remember his name—laying his hand on my forehead and saying Heinrich Karl, but I can't bring back the last name."

The doctor interrupted, "Well, that is a start now, isn't it? What else do you remember?"

"Well, that's where it gets strange. Susan and I are friends. I like her a lot and I think she likes me, but back in the depths of my mind, there have been thoughts that maybe somewhere there is this girl that might be waiting for me. Now, on the way home from church, I had this name that came up. Katy. I don't know how she fits. I also have a feeling, an almost memory, of terrible dread. The feeling could almost be classed as paranoia. I don't know how to handle that," John confessed.

"It seems that you may be on the verge of that breakthrough that I promised you so long ago. Just keep doing what you have been and come back to see me in a month. Take this chart up and hand it to the nurse on the way out."

With that, the doctor got up and headed for the door.

John hadn't told the Wheelers yet of what had happened when he went with Susan to Charleston. They were hinting that it might be a good time for him to be baptized and he didn't have the heart to tell them just yet he was definitely a Lutheran. He knew that he would have to sit down with George soon and tell him. As it stood, he was to get another Sunday off in a week and that meant if the weather was good Susan and he would make a fast round trip to Redeemer Lutheran in Charleston. Since he had been working Sundays, Susan had not been going to church with the Wheelers anyway. He still went Sunday nights and on Wednesday nights, but that was more out of respect for George and Beth than for his spiritual health and growth. On the next trip to Charleston, he wanted to talk to the pastor about taking Communion. Instinctively, he knew it would be at Redeemer, in the comfort of his tradition, where his spiritual growth would come.

May and June passed quickly and here he was Monday night, July 4th, after the fireworks at the softball park, lying in his bed just trying to wind down. Tomorrow morning would come soon and he had to be ready. As he said his evening prayers, he prayed for Susan, her family, his family—wherever they were—and his friends and neighbors in Williamson. Then came blessed sleep.

CHAPTER 13

Sunday, August 14th found John and Susan making the drive to visit her folks in Wisconsin. John was due for a vacation and had two weeks he could take. Susan actually had three weeks that she could have taken, but chose to take only two.

Susan had not been back to visit since she took the position in Williamson almost two years ago. During that time, her parents, being tied to milking the cows and just keeping up with the crops, had not found the time to come to Williamson to visit her. She, having just found her wings, felt no desire to make the trip back until now. She felt she needed to keep her independence! She was settled and confident, a different person.

Now she felt the time was right to go back. This was the first time in her twenty-six years she had ever considered driving such a long way alone! The more she thought about it, the more this became a very exciting trip for her, but the thought of such a long drive also was rather daunting. The other side of her worried a little! *What would she do if she ran into trouble? Was a girl traveling alone vulnerable? She knew she was brave, but was she that brave? She didn't know.* Her parents suggested she take the bus to Janesville and they would meet her there. Actually, her father had had a heated discussion with her on the phone on that very subject. She had left Wisconsin to spread her wings and win her freedom and now they wanted her to take a bus! No! She was going to do this her way! The stubborn streak her father accused her of having was pushing her to make the drive just to show them it could be done! The question now was how to feel secure while she was doing this.

After much thought, her answer to all of this was John. After all, he was her best friend. They were so much alike in the way they spoke and felt about things. He always treated her with respect and she had learned to trust him. And she had romantic feelings for him. She hoped he also had these kinds of feelings for her, but he was always so timid, or even guarded, in how he showed whatever feelings he had. Did she trust him enough to make a two week trip with him? Yes. They were attending church together and he always acted like a gentleman and treated her like a lady.

It was in the middle of July when she mustered up the courage to ask him if he would make the trip with her. She noted it took a week for him to get back with his answer. She assumed it took him that long to get his vacation request approved.

John was surprised when Susan asked him if he would accompany her on her trip. They had talked several times about her going and he had encouraged her to make the trip. He had even helped her plan the route she would take.

He assumed she would be making the drive alone and it never occurred to him she would ask him to come along. He had to take time to think this through. His love for Susan was growing, but since his memory had begun to come back he knew his name, it was Heinrich Karl, and he had these snatches of remembered feelings for a Katy. He was concerned because he feared falling in love with Susan and then finding out he was committed to someone else. He pondered this dilemma. He analyzed the feelings he felt and his symptoms matched those he read about in the love stories in the books from the library. He had these feelings, but he couldn't show them until he found out who this Katy was and if he had made some commitment to her. Why was he so melancholy when he thought of her?

He had almost turned Susan down. He didn't want to hurt her, but he was afraid of sharing the confusion he felt about Katy with her. Susan made a pretty good argument for his coming along. After all, he recognized the fact that she is a pretty girl taking her first long driving trip and agreed that her argument about a girl being vulnerable alone in the car did make sense. It wasn't like she was driving around Williamson or Mingo County.

He took a week to make up his mind to go. During that time, he had another scheduled appointment with the doctor. They discussed his progress and what new things he had remembered since the last visit. Together, they delved into the sketchy memories of this Katy person. The doctor reviewed with him the profile he had made from what he observed and recommended that John take the trip.

"It might bring back more memories," he said.

He also told John to look at the tobacco grown in Kentucky on his way. Seeing as he knew so much about growing it, just seeing it might spark some memories. In the end, the doctor reinforced his recommendation that John take the trip, stating, "Have a safe trip and tell me what you found when I see you next month."

John measured the pros and cons about this trip and in the end decided to go with her. The two things that tipped the scale were: the doctor recommended the trip, and she needed a companion. When he told her, he said he was *honored* to be asked and would go.

Now they were on their way. The route they had chosen took them through the mountains of Eastern Kentucky to Lexington. The roads improved from Lexington through Louisville to Indianapolis. From Indianapolis, they decided to angle west to take U. S. 41 up to Gary, Indiana, and then take US Hwy 14 north out of Chicago to Janesville, Wisconsin. The plan called for a stopover in Indianapolis. The one thing her father insisted on, and she did, was to book two rooms in the Howard Johnson Motel in Indianapolis. He didn't want his daughter staying in some *flee infested* motel.

They started driving early in the morning and made it to Indianapolis by four in the afternoon. After a good meal at the Howard Johnson's Restaurant, they said goodnight and each went to their rooms. After an early breakfast, they were again on their way. They made it to Chicago by noon and pulled into the driveway of the Radke farm in time for the afternoon/evening chores.

The Radke farm was about three miles west of Milton Junction just off US Highway 59 near County Road N. The farm buildings were about two hundred feet back from the road and consisted of an old farmhouse with a large, two car garage next to it, a very large modern barn with three Harvestor brand glass silos, a large milkhouse/pumphouse, and a large machine shed.

Susan drove her car into the driveway and parked it on the concrete apron in front of the garage door farther from the side door to the house.

"This is it!" she exclaimed as she opened her door to get out.

John opened his door, stood up, and looked around. "This looks like a big operation."

"Com'on inside and meet my mother," insisted an excited Susan as she headed for the side door.

John followed her into the entryway of the house. This was a little room containing a small sink, clothes hooks, and a chair where they might change clothes and wash their hands when they came in from the fields. As he came through another door into the large farm kitchen, he heard Susan's mother let out a scream of surprise.

"Hi, Mom. We made it home!" Susan joyfully announced.

"You shouldn't do that to your mother. My heart is going a mile a minute," she said as she hugged Susan.

"Mother, I want you to meet the John Rockhouse I have told you so much about. John, meet Esther Radke, my mother. Mom, meet John."

Esther Radke was a tall woman, almost six feet tall by John's reckoning. From the picture Susan had showed him, he expected to see a much heavier woman, but she was very thin and graceful. She had a pleasant face with stunning blue eyes and rosy cheeks. John could see where Susan got her eyes. Her blond hair, which showed no signs yet of graying, formed a halo, like he had seen in so many religious paintings, around her face.

"It is so good to meet Susan's friends," Esther said as she came over and surprised John with a great big hug. "Did you enjoy the trip?"

The hug took John by surprise as he tried to answer her.

"Yes," he stammered back.

"I didn't see dad when I drove in. Where is he?" Susan asked.

"The day has been cool, so he has been up in the haymow restacking hay bales to make room for next cutting. Your brother probably took Corky to the back pasture with him to get the cows. Corky will be very glad to see you. Every now and then he finds something of yours and goes around the house sniffing for you," her mother explained.

It took John a minute or two to realize Corky was the family dog.

"You didn't tell me about your dog," John said.

"Well, he really is my brother's dog, but I did play with him a lot," Susan responded.

Esther had gone over to the side door and was calling to her husband in the barn that it was time for him to come in. She said to Susan, "You really should have hid the car so you could surprise your father too."

"He probably won't even notice it," Susan replied.

"We have made a few changes around here since you left. Come and I'll show you," she stated as she led them into the dining room. "I convinced Dad the old dining room set was just too small for all the "get to-gathers" since the grammas and the grampas have stopped holding the family diners for Thanksgiving, Christmas, New Year's, and Easter. After Easter last year, he agreed with me and this is the new set. Now come into the living room. We got a Zenith twenty-three-inch consol TV with the remote on/off, channel, and sound control."

She picked up a little box and, with a clicking sound, turned on the TV.

Just then, they heard a voice in the kitchen calling out, "Mom, where are you?"

"I was just in the living room showing off the new TV," she called back. They turned and started back to the kitchen, arriving just as a man stepped out of the door after washing his hands. From the picture he had seen of William, John expected him to be a big man, but big didn't describe William Radke. He was over six feet tall and had to be at least 275 pounds of muscle.

"Susan, you look well-fed and healthy for being away from your mother's cooking for so long," her dad said with a smile as he placed his right hand on her shoulder and greeted her in his stiff Prussian manner.

"You look pretty good yourself. Dad, I want you to meet John Rockhouse," she replied. She then stepped over to where John was standing and said, "John, meet William Radke, my dad."

John instinctively made a slight bowing movement and reached out to shake Mr. Radke's hand.

"Pleased to meet you, sir."

William Radke extended his hand and said, "Good to meet you," as they shook hands. "By the way, you can call me Bill."

"Will and Corky just drove the cows into the barnyard. Dad, you better get out there and open the barn door before all sixty of them begin to moo," Esther commanded and then said to John, "They get pretty rambunctious if you don't open that door fast enough. They want to get to the grist in the feeder in front of their stanchion and then they want to be milked."

"I understand," John answered. "I have a vague memory of something like that. Would you have some work clothes that would fit me? I would like to go out and help."

From some part of his brain came the memory of just what had to be done to milk the cows and he wanted to help.

"You don't have to go out there. We don't expect guests to help," counseled Esther.

"I really would like to. I think I can fit in a shirt and trousers that Bill wears if we roll up the sleeves and pants legs. These are work boots and I can always clean them later," he pleaded.

"I'll go get some clothes but we will try Will's on you. He is much smaller than Dad," Esther replied as she headed toward the laundry room.

Susan came over close to John and gave him a little hug.

"That is so sweet of you to volunteer to help."

"I know I have done this before. I know how. It will be fun to help around here while we are here."

Just then, Esther came back with the work clothes. John took them into the entry way and changed.

"How do I look?" he asked them.

"Just like a farmer," Susan replied.

John went out to the barn where he met Will and helped with the chores and the milking.

"He looks like a nice boy," Esther said to Susan.

"He has become my best friend in Williamson. Being different is not easy to overcome in West Virginia. However, I have made some acquaintances and the people at Redeemer Lutheran in Charleston are very friendly. I guess in areas where there are few Lutherans, we all stick closer together just like family," she answered.

Susan and her mother continued to talk about the life Susan was leading in West Virginia and how she enjoyed her work, but Susan never answered her mother's probing inquiries into the depth of the relationship between John and herself.

It took them an hour to milk the sixty cows and another half hour to do the rest of the chores, so it was close to seven when the three men were back in the house for supper.

They spent the rest of the evening just sitting around the kitchen table talking. Mostly, the family was just helping Susan catch up on all that had happened around the farm and the town since she left. John sat quietly, listening to all the old news and all the shared memories. Deep in his heart, he wondered where his family was and when, if ever, he would spend a night catching up like this.

Around nine thirty, as the light was finally fading to darkness, someone made a comment to the effect that five thirty comes soon and they all went to bed. Will and Susan went upstairs to their bedrooms and John was made comfortable on the living room sofa. As he said his prayers and went to sleep, he kind of missed the horn of the evening train and the squeaking of the train wheels as they rounded the bend coming into Williamson.

One day melted into another as he worked around the farm and got to know Susan and her family better.

CHAPTER 14

Sunday, August 21 began as a bright, cloudless summer day, the kind that made you just want to sit around the house and relax. John, Susan and her family went to early church at St. Paul's in Janesville and by ten thirty were back at the farm to do what they wanted.

Susan had plans. She wanted to drive to Madison and show John the Wisconsin State Capital. She thought this would be a great outing. Her mom, dad, and brother had hinted at making this a family outing, but she had other ideas. Really, she was a little frustrated. She wanted sometime alone with John. So far this week, there was always someone that would get between them and they hardly had any time alone together to talk. And when they did, the subject never got around to just them. She wanted John alone. She wanted to get close, but John seemed so stiff, so *Prussian*. Just like her dad.

This week had not gone well for John. The more he worked around the farm, the more memories came back to him. He was vaguely familiar with this area. He knew too much about Janesville. He knew where the Sears store was. For some strange reason, he was familiar with the GM Fisher Body Plant there. Why did he know so much about Mercy Hospital? He knew the Rock River. He even thought he had fished on it.

He had more memories of Katy, and these memories were of love and desire. But the memories were like in a dream. They would begin and then morph into something else. They were never complete. This week also showed him the side of Susan that he had begun to fall in love with. She was sweet, industrious, caring, and a hard worker. She was everything a man like him could want in a wife, but there was his past. Katy was hanging ominously over his head.

Susan had been trying to get him alone all week; at least that was what it looked like to John. In his current state of mind, he felt he just couldn't be alone with her. Luckily, her brother was on him like a shadow and they had become great friends.

Susan wanted to go for a ride, just the two of them. This was going to be one hard ride to take. He was going to have to tell her about Katy. He was going to have to tell her that until he knew more about his previous life he would have to put his feelings for her aside. This was going to be tough, but it had to be done. The pastor had a place in this morning's sermon that dealt with how we must be open and honest with the people we love. Maybe this would be the way he could bring up the subject.

They waved good-bye to her family and began to drive north on Highway 59 to Edgerton, where they would pick up Highway 51 to Madison.

As soon as they got on the road, John began to recognize things. Landmarks he couldn't ignore.

"Susan, what do you know about me really?" John questioned.

"I know you are reliable, honest, trustworthy, and my best friend," she replied.

"But my background, what do you know about that?" he asked.

"I know what was written on your hospital chart, which wasn't much. I know what you have told me. I know you are now remembering things," she replied.

"I have begun to remember so much more since we have arrived. I don't know where this will lead. In his sermon, Pastor Kuhn talked about being honest with the people you love. I placed you in that category. I like you a lot. You have been the best friend I could ever have had and you have helped me through a very rough time," he said slowly, carefully picking is words.

"You have helped me an awful lot. You have no idea what it was like to leave my home and follow a dream. Working three to eleven is not the best way to meet new people either. The nurses I work with are older and I just don't fit in with them, my attitudes are different. My farming background is so much different. I love the mountains, I really do, but I grew up a flatlander and I am different. My landlady has been no help in introducing me into the community. I endured for almost a year. The last thing I wanted to do was go back to Wisconsin defeated, so I stuck it out. I always looked forward to seeing you, and then you were discharged. Even in your confusion, you reminded me of home, the way you spoke and your accent. When you came to work at the hospital I knew I had someone who could be a real friend. We have so much in common! Your introducing me to the Wheelers gave me a family in Williamson. Your going to church with me, all of this has changed my life. I think I love you," she tearfully explained as she reached over to hold his hand.

Her last statement was too much for John to handle at the moment. He felt her warm hand in his, he heard the tenderness in her voice. He had to respond, but how could he with what was on his mind. "I think I love you too, but there is something I must tell you."

"Not now," she said. "Not now."

They rode quietly for a while, when all of a sudden, John excitedly announced, "I know where I am! I remember these roads. I think I know my way home. I will tell you where to turn and if things have not changed a lot in the last two years, I will find the farm!"

"John, that's wonderful!" Susan exclaimed.

"What if there is someone there waiting for me? What will you do?" John asked.

"What do you mean?" Susan worriedly asked.

"I mean what if there has been someone waiting there for me all this time?" John lowered his voice as he spoke seriously to her. "If there is a girlfriend or a wife, we have to prepare for that possibility."

Susan became very somber and looked straight at the road and asked, "What makes you think that could happen?"

"I remember a name, a name that has brought up very lonely feelings, feelings of dread. Her name is Katy. There is something there; I just can't find what it is," he carefully answered.

They drove on for a while in silence.

John read the sign that stated Edgerton City Limits, Population 4,256 and announced, "We are here in Edgerton. We have to turn right at the light and go north on Highway 51."

Susan nervously commented on the small farms and gave a running commentary on farm life in southern Wisconsin. John sat there listening and not wanting to tell Susan that what she was saying was exactly what he could have told her. The traffic on Highway 51 was light as they drove north through Albion and on toward Stoughton. Just as they got close to Stoughton, John recognized a road. It was marked County Road N.

"Turn here," he suddenly instructed. "It shouldn't be far now, only a few miles."

Susan obediently slowed way down and made the turn. She had a feeling of trepidation as she sat silently behind the wheel and drove slowly up the road. The landscape had become hilly. As John excitedly watched the farms go by he was looking for the little side road that would lead to the farm where he grew up.

"What time is it?" he asked.

Susan looked at her nurse's watch and answered, "A little before noon."

"Over the next hill should be a little road. We will turn right when we get to it," John announced.

"I see it." Susan responded as she slowed the car to make the turn.

They drove down the road about a mile and came to a mail box. The name on the box was Warnke.

"Turn in here," instructed a suddenly excited and emotional Heinrich Karl Warnke. John finally knew his last name! All the frustration and longing from since the accident found an emotional release and he burst out in tears. He sat on his side of the car joyfully sobbing. "I can remember, I can remember," and he kept on repeating it.

Susan stopped the car in the driveway and looked through her open car window at the screen door that led into the side of the house. Through the window to the left side of the door, she saw a gray haired old woman pull back the sheer white curtain to get a better look at the car that that was parked in the driveway at the side of her house. Susan knew that she probably could not see clearly to the other side of the car at the weeping man who sat next to her.

Susan sat in the car looking at the door. Eventually, it opened and a tall, lean, rugged-looking old man with snow white hair came slowly down the steps and down the sidewalk, which led to her car door.

"Can I help you?" he inquired as he leaned down beside the car window to speak to her. He had not leaned down far enough to get a full view of the sobbing passenger.

The nurse in Susan took over and, as shaken as she was by John's/Henry's immediate reaction to the sudden flood of memory in the last few moments, looked up at the man and said, "I think I have someone in the car with me who wants to see you. I know you will want to see him." With that, she opened the car door and got out.

Henry's sobbing abated as she left the car and closed the door. She took the man by the arm and together they walked around the back of the car to the passenger's door.

She opened the door and the man looked in seeing John Rockhouse/Heinrich Karl with his face cradled in his hands still sitting in the car. She reached in and moved John's hands. The man gasped as he recognized the face of the man before him and turned as white as a ghost as he grabbed onto the car for support.

From the house, an old lady's voice called out, "Is everything all right out there?"

It was answered by the pale man who called, "Helen, come out here quick! It's Henry. I think he is hurt!"

Susan reached in, and in a comforting way, slowly helped Henry get himself out of the front seat of the car into a standing position. Facing his father, he exclaimed excitedly, "Dad, I'm home!"

By this time, Helen, a white-haired old woman with a round, pleasant face, having moved as fast as a large heavy woman in her mid sixties could, had reached the side of the car. Helen, having heard Henry's name and seeing Henry standing beside the car, was herself looking a little pale as she rushed forward, threw her arms around her son, and asked. "Henry, are you all right?"

Susan stepped back and made room for the man to come closer and wrap his arms around them both.

Henry still looked shaken, but slowly pulled himself together and in a quivering voice said, "I'm glad to be home," as the three of them stood in such an embrace.

Henry was being hugged by his mother, something that had not happened since he was a little kid and his father was a part of that hug and Henry had never seen his father hug his mother. This wasn't how he was brought up! Henry felt overwhelmed by the emotion of the moment and the memories that flooded back to him. The overpowering emotion was so hard to control. It was love for and from his parents, knowing who he is and who he was, and bringing the two lives together and finally knowing why he felt the way he felt about Katy.

Susan leaned against the front fender of the car and looked at them. She had never seen anything like this before. The return of a lost son was foreign to anything she could have imagined. She felt happiness for John, no, Henry. She was going to have to become used to calling him that, and his family.

She felt love for Henry right now that she had no way to express. *Was there any future with him? Why am I standing here like a dope? I'm in the way! I have to do something! I'll just walk*, she thought, and she began to move away from the car. She hadn't taken more than five steps toward the barn when she felt a strong hand on her shoulder.

Henry had come to himself and suddenly noticed Susan looking dejected leaning against the fender of the car and then turning to walk away.

"I have to do something," he had quickly whispered to his parents. "Susan," he quietly pleaded as he placed his hand on her shoulder, "please come here. I want to introduce you to my mom and dad."

Susan turned slowly as he caught up to her. She wanted so badly to put her arms around him and give him a big hug and she wanted him to hold her tight, but none of that happened. Instead, she took hold of his outstretched hand and followed him back to where his folks were standing beside the car.

"Mom and Dad, I want you to meet the one person in my life I hold dearest, Susan Radke. Susan, this is Dad and Mom, ah, Fred and Helen Warnke," he said, sweeping his arm in a presenting gesture.

Susan stood there not knowing what to do, but immediately Helen moved to her and wrapped her arms around her in a strong hug. Fred came to her and grasped her hand in a firm, welcoming handshake.

"We should go in the house where we can sit down and my, my, have you eaten dinner yet?" Helen asked excitedly as they began to walk up the path to the house. Helen was in shock, Henry was back, her prayers answered, but what should she do? She was so confused. Instinctively she turned to food.

"Why, no," Henry admitted.

"We were just sitting down to dinner when you drove in," Helen responded still confused.

"Why didn't you call ahead so I could have prepared something?"

"This will make no sense to you, but Susan wanted to show me the Capital in Madison," Henry tried to explain.

"But you have been going there since you were a little kid!" exclaimed Helen, disbelieving what she had just heard.

Susan looked at both Fred and Helen and said, "We have a long story to tell you."

They climbed the steps and entered the kitchen. They all seemed to stand around as though no one knew what to say or do. Susan concluded that Fred and Helen were in some state of shock at suddenly seeing Henry after such a long time with no news. Henry was still John, coping with being Henry, and still adjusting. It seemed as though this was taking a long time to sink in or they couldn't believe what had just happened. It was as if they were slowly going through the motions of walking and breathing without knowing what to say or do.

Helen began fidgeting with the dinner she was preparing. It was as though, by some miracle, she could stretch the small plate of cheese and cold-cuts to feed four instead of just the two of them as was planned. She fumbled around, taking things out of the refrigerator, looking at them, and putting them back.

Fred was walking around the table, shaking his head and rearranging the chairs, pulling them out from under the table and then putting them back.

Henry just kind of paced, looking down at the worn linoleum on the floor, not knowing where to begin to tell them what had happened.

Susan was doing her best to cope with this situation herself. She was here with John Rockhouse, who now was Henry Warnke, who had parents as old-looking as her grandparents and nobody was coping with this situation well at all. His parents looked as though they had seen a ghost. They needed time. They needed time together. She needed time!

Fred eventually sat down by the table.

"Mrs. Warnke, can I help you in any way with dinner?" asked Susan quietly.

This question seemed to break Helen's mood. She looked over at Susan and spoke apologetically, "I have nothing prepared to feed you."

"Can you make peanut butter and jelly sandwiches?" Susan asked.

"Henry just came home I can't give him just peanut butter and jelly sandwiches. I have to feed him," she replied with a quiver in her voice that indicated she was almost in tears.

Fred sat there as though he were stunned.

"Mother, please sit down and let me see if I can find the peanut butter and jelly for the sandwiches. With those and what is already on the table, that should be enough for dinner," Henry suggested as he got up and led his mother to a chair at the table near where his father sat. "Susan, there should be a knife in that drawer to the right of the sink. I will get the rest and we will make sandwiches."

With that said, they began preparing the extra portions for the meal.

Fred was getting some color back in his face and Helen seemed to have calmed down a bit as they sat down at the table to eat.

Fred led by folding his hands and bowing his head and everyone around the table followed suit.

"God is great, God is good, let us thank him for this food, and let us thank him for the safe return of Henry to us. Amen."

Susan looked up and saw that with that simple table prayer the whole perspective around the table had changed. There seemed to be a look of joy showing on Helen's face, a look of peace on Fred's, and Henry's face no longer had that look of confusion she had seen so often for so long.

"Where have you been and why haven't you contacted us until now?" Fred asked in a calm, but reprimanding voice. In his mind, he was really asking, *Why have you not been in touch for almost two years?*

Henry looked up at his father, then his mother, and turned his head to look at Susan and began.

"I was in an accident, a very bad accident. I lost my memory. I didn't know who I was or where I was from. Susan here has done more for me than all the doctors and the medicine combined."

"I never did like that motorcycle. I knew it would be the death of you!" Helen said with conviction.

"Mother, I sold the motorcycle. I don't yet remember all the details, but this happened in a car," he explained.

"Where did this happen and why weren't we notified? They surely could have traced that back to us." Fred continued.

Tears came to Henry's eyes as he answered. "The car burned and everything inside was lost except for a scrap of paper that indicated I had just bought the car. There was nothing to go on."

With this statement, Susan saw his mother's face turn ashen and she rushed to her side to steady her. With a second shock like this, Susan was afraid this old lady might have a heart attack, so she tried to do what she could.

Fred sat there stunned.

Silence followed as Henry's parents again adjusted to the new information and began to cope. Just to calm her, Susan stood by Helen, her hands massaging her shoulders.

Henry continued, "I was in traction in the hospital for eight weeks with a broken leg and then spent another six months in a cast. I now have a job at the hospital and am paying off the debt I owe. I only got my memory back a few minutes ago as Susan was driving me to Madison. If I could have, I would have let you know right away."

"When did this happen?" Fred asked in a low voice.

"Friday night, October 23rd, the year I left home," he said grimly.

"We got your last letter some time around there and then the letters stopped. We didn't know what to think. Mom kept blaming that motorcycle and saying something had happened. I kept telling her no news is good news. We wanted to go and visit you in Huntington, but the farm kept us tied down until after Thanksgiving. I sold the cows after you left. They were just too much for me to handle. I saved the money for your share, though. Anyway, the tobacco wasn't cured good enough to start stripping yet, so we had Walter look after the place and went looking for you in Huntington."

Susan was still standing with Helen. Henry had his head cradled in his hands. No one had taken a bite to eat yet.

"We got to Huntington and went to the address we had and they told us you had just moved and hadn't given them a forwarding address yet. We checked with the pastor at the church you wrote us you attended and he said that you told him you were moving to a new place for the winter, but you never gave him an address and when you stopped coming, he thought you had moved somewhere else or gone back to Wisconsin. We spent two days looking for you with no luck and came home. All that was left was hope and we prayed," his father told him gravely.

By this time, Helen had her color back again and Susan had returned to her place at the table.

"How are Walter, Sarah, and the boys?" Henry asked to change the subject.

"Walter is still building Chevys at Fisher Body, although the drive is starting to get to him. Sarah is the same as always, and the boys are in with grandpa here working the tobacco on shares," Helen admitted enthusiastically. "Dad isn't as young as he used to be, so this has helped a lot. You're leaving really put a strain on him."

"Now, Mom, you know that ain't true. I'm as good as I ever was," Fred said with conviction.

"Let's eat. I'm starving," Susan said.

"Good idea," Fred was quick to say.

During the rest of the meal, Fred and Helen told Henry and Susan what things had happened since he left. Henry sat quietly and listened. Susan had nothing to add, so she quietly ate her one peanut butter and jelly sandwich. It didn't take long to finish the meal.

When dinner was done, Henry, who had been more and more moody as the meal wore on, got up and announced, "I have to take a walk. It may take me a while."

With that, he left the house and headed back into the hills behind the barn.

"He was like that all spring the year he left. Maybe you can snap him out of it," Fred confided to Susan.

Helen got up from the table and began clearing the dishes away.

CHAPTER 15

After Henry left for his walk, Fred announced: "I just can't sit around. I have to keep busy, I have to think, I have to do something. I'm going out in the tobacco field and prepare an acre or two of tobacco for harvesting."

"Aren't you going to call Walter and tell him the good news?" Helen asked.

"We'll call him later tonight. I think they were going someplace today. That's why we didn't see them in church," Fred informed her.

Susan was left alone in the house with Helen.

Helen was sitting at the kitchen table in what looked like deep thought. She didn't say anything; she acted as if she were a statue just gazing off into space. This whole scene had taken on a dream-like quality.

Susan asked anxiously, "Helen, are you all right?"

Helen gave no answer.

"I think I will go outside and get a breath of air," Susan said as she headed toward the door.

This day was one of those nice, mild, lazy summer days with the temperature in the mid seventies, when just sitting outside of the house in the shade was very relaxing. The kitchen door had been left open when Henry went through it. She opened the screen door, stepped outside, and sat on the steps leading up to the door.

She looked toward the barn, toward the direction John, no, Henry—it was so hard to call him Henry because he was John for so long, she just needed time—had taken when he headed out to think. She studied the farmyard where he had lived. The land here was more hilly than where she had grown up. The farms seemed smaller too. There was the red barn, not big enough to hold more than thirty cows. Toward the rear of the barn, she could see the barnyard where the cows had come when it was milking time. At the end of the barn was a tall cast concrete silo, looking gray and weathered. There was the tobacco shed painted red like the barn. It was about thirty feet wide and about 120 feet long. There was an older building with large doors that must be the machine shed, although there were two tractors and some wagons parked on the grass in the yard near it. This operation looked a lot smaller than her folks'. She sat there on the steps for a while wondering what was going to happen next. Would Henry stay here and she go back to Milton alone tonight? Would Henry stay here and let her go back to Williamson alone?

She didn't know what to think. After a little while, she heard Helen making noise with the dishes inside the house, so she went back inside to help clean up.

"I guess Henry couldn't tell you about his family when he couldn't remember. You must be curious and wondering about us. I don't know where to start," Helen said hesitatingly as she tried to collect her thoughts.

"I took care of him when he first came to the hospital. I guess we just were comfortable together," Susan volunteered.

"You're not from there are you?" Helen probed. "You don't talk like them."

"I'm from over in Milton. My folks have a farm there. We milk sixty cows now, but that number goes up and down," Susan replied.

"My, my, you grew up so close to us," Helen stated in surprise.

"Yeah, but it was a county away," she mused.

"How did you end up in Williamson?" Helen inquired.

"When I graduated from nursing school, I was adventurous and wanted to work away from where I grew up. I took a nursing position in Williamson. This was the first chance I had to come home and visit my folks. I didn't want to drive the long distance alone, so I asked Henry to come with me. Henry and I have been close friends; we go to the Lutheran church in Charleston together and we both like to take little side trips in the area. Henry's doctor has been trying to bring back Henry's memory the whole time. He tried to generate a profile to determine where Henry grew up to jog his memory. So far, the only things Henry's doctor has guessed right are that he must have come from the Midwest and that he might be Lutheran. Henry's finding his way home today was a complete surprise," Susan explained.

"And he couldn't remember!" was all Helen could say.

Susan thought for a moment and began asking questions.

"Can you tell me about Henry? Why did he leave home? Was he always so solemn? What would have made him leave the table and go for a walk? Henry was telling me about some memories he couldn't quite bring up concerning a girl. Is there someone I should know about?"

"Henry has always been a sensitive boy. I guess you could say he grew up as an only child, although he has an older brother, Walter. Maybe it would make more sense if I start at the beginning. Fred and I were childhood sweethearts. We met at church and married young. We were married in 1921 and Walter was born in 1922, two weeks before our first wedding anniversary. Henry was born in 1940 when I was thirty-seven. He was just a baby when the war started in 1940. He never got to know his older brother until after the war. Walter grew up patriotic and joined the Navy right after Pearl Harbor in 1941. After the war, Walter never lived here again. During the war, he and his old girlfriend kept in touch, became engaged, and during his furlough, married. She lived with her folks. When he came back after the war, they rented a house. He went to work in Janesville at Fisher Body and when they saved enough money, they bought a house. He lives not too far from here and now his sons help us a lot on the farm.

Henry thought Walter was an uncle until he was about ten years old. Walter's wedding picture with him in uniform was always on the mantle, of course, but Henry didn't understand Walter was his brother until he came across some old pictures of Walter when he was a boy," Helen explained.

"That's sad," Susan commented.

"I suppose I should tell you what drove Henry away from home," she stated in a sad voice. "I doubt that Henry will be able to tell you himself."

"Was it bad?" Susan asked anxiously.

"Yes, it was bad," Helen said gravely. "But I guess I should start at the beginning. During the war, we sheltered Henry from all the news about the war. With all the killing that was taking place, we wanted him to grow up without the worry. Walter was fighting in the Pacific, we never knew where, but ships were being sunk and we never knew when we would get the news of his being lost. We did a lot of praying. We just wanted Henry to grow up not knowing the fear we felt. When we butchered, we made sure he was away from the farm with one of his grandmas so he didn't see the animals being killed. We tried to encourage his Christian faith. We impressed on him early on that we were Lutheran and told him why we were Lutheran. We read the Bible to him and we went to church.

Right after the war, I think it was 1946, when he was six, the farm next to ours was sold to a Catholic family by the name of Collins. They seemed to be very nice people and they had a large family, three boys and two girls. Their youngest child, Katy, was much younger than the rest of the children. Having a lot of kids was good if you were a farming family. They moved in during the end of February and we became neighbors. In a farming community like ours, we don't have a lot of free time for socializing, so most of our close friends are the people we see at church. Back then, this area had a lot of Lutheran families and most of us went to the same Lutheran church. They were about the only Catholic family in the community. They socialized mainly with the people who attended their church. So, other than in community endeavors such as the school Mother's Club or the thrashing crew, although they lived on the farm next door, we had no real regular contact with them."

"It was pretty much that way with us over in Milton too," Susan was quick to say.

Helen continued telling her story. "In those days, all our children went to a one-room, eighth grade school out here in the country. No child had to walk over a mile and a half. Then, after eighth grade, the kids went to Stoughton for high school. The bus came around and picked them up."

"We all went to the combined grade school in Milton," Susan chimed in.

"Because of how his birthday fell, Henry was six when he entered first grade. Katy Collins from next door was the only other first grader that year. The two of them hit it off and became great friends when they were at school, but as you might guess our two families were never close.

Matter of fact, there was always a little competition between Fred and Paul Collins. We milked cows then and shipped our milk to the Chicago Market. The Milk Inspectors would come around on a regular basis to certify that the milk produced would be 'pure.' Once a year, they would rate the farms accordingly. Dad always took pride in how his barn and milk-house were kept and, for many years, was one of the highest rated farms in the area. The rivalry for the number one farm was with Paul Collins, who had it in his mind that his rating should be higher than Dad's. Dad never took it personal, but the rivalry was always an undercurrent between them.

Henry and Katy, though, were oblivious to the realities of that aspect of farm life. They were very close in first grade. We were glad Henry had someone his age in the school with him.

They didn't seem so close for a while in second grade, but in third grade Katy was the only person Henry talked about. Of course, when they were both ten years old, they joined the 4-H Club. That was when Fred and I became aware just how close they had become. Now, don't get me wrong, we don't hate Catholics, but we are Lutheran. In those days, when a Catholic married a person of another faith, the Catholic Church required the non-Catholic to sign a paper stating that the kids would be brought up Catholic. No Lutheran parent wanted his or her future grandchildren brought up Catholic. We tried to instill in the children the notion that if you wanted to marry a Catholic, you better have that person convert before the wedding. The other option was to discourage our kids from dating a Catholic.

It seems the Collins's felt the same way about Lutherans and were doing their best to instill the Catholic approach to dating in their kids too. Looking back at it, at least we had something in common with them," Helen told her seriously.

"I think you were very successful in instilling the Lutheran traditions and faith in Henry," Susan commented.

"We did our best to keep him in the church," Helen replied.

"I grew up Lutheran and my first year in Williamson I really missed my church. I tried the Episcopal Church and some others, but I had to find a Missouri Lutheran church. The closest one was in Charleston, ninety miles away. After Thanksgiving that year, I was in the Christmas Spirit one day, humming *Silent Night* when I entered Henry's room and it was from his deepest memories that Henry remembered the words in German. You can't imagine how that felt to be able to sing *Silent Night* in German with him. I then tried humming tunes from the Lutheran hymnal page-five liturgy, and from his deep memories of the faith you instilled in him, he was able to sing the responses with me. He remembered those when he remembered nothing else. But the real question is what made him forget?" Susan asked grimly.

"I can't answer that," Helen pointed out. "All I can tell you is what happened. Anyway, we knew they were best friends, but we never worried about them falling in love. They were just kids. We concluded that, given time, the attraction would wear off. But when they were in the same 4-H Club, we began to notice them sitting and working together and for the first time saw how close they had become. We tried to do things to broaden his group of friends. His older brother Walter's oldest kid was ten years younger than Henry and the others had even a greater gulf. As much as we tried to bring them together, they never became close.

The only person his age was Katy. I guess the Collins's had the same problem with Katy and the kids were just close. Both we and the Collins's could see what was happening, but neither of us thought it would ever get as serious as it became."

"Is he still in love with her?" asked a worried Susan.

"I suppose in some ways he still is," Helen confirmed. "But let me continue. There is this majestic oak tree that straddles the fence line between the Collins farm and ours. That tree must be over one hundred years old. The way it is positioned in the hill, it isn't usually seen from either farmyard. The kids found that tree one summer. When they were done with their chores, they would meet under that tree each on their side of the fence and talk. We didn't realize that they had gotten in the habit of meeting there. When we found out about it, we gave up. The Collins's seemed to have done the same.

When we went looking for Henry in the evenings when the chores were done, that was where we would find them. That is probably where you will find Henry now. Anyway, we just gave up and hoped his faith would see him through this.

I think things kind of cooled the two years he was in confirmation class, but he was confirmed in eighth grade in the spring and that year, although he was well-schooled in his knowledge of doctrine, he still had this attraction for Katy."

"They started high school that fall. Henry met some other kids and they had a group that chummed around together. We didn't hear much about Katy. Nobody in that group was allowed to date. But I guess Henry and Katy still met at the old tree, but they were both kept busy and we more or less forgot about them being together.

By this time, Henry was raising cattle for his 4-H projects. The objective was to show these cattle at the County 4-H Fair and win a blue ribbon for the best animal. When he was sixteen, he could spend the night with his cattle in the cattle barn. That year, Henry was showing a Guernsey milk cow and a Heifer. Katy was showing two Heifers. She also was spending the nights in the barn. Being in the same Club, their animals were tied in adjacent stalls. They spent the week grooming their Heifers and competing in the show ring for ribbons. Although only one got the blue ribbon, the experience seemed to have brought them closer together. From then on, they started officially going together.

He bought his high school Class of "58" class ring so she could wear it. There was the prom. Whenever possible, they spent their study time together. They graduated and each made plans for where they were going to go to school."

Susan got up from her chair and went over to the kitchen sink, picked up a glass from the counter, and got a drink of cold water. "Do you want a drink?" she asked.

"No thank you," Helen quietly stated as she continued the story. "Katy decided she would go to become a nurse. She was accepted at St. Mary's Hospital School of Nursing in Milwaukee where she would start in the fall."

"I knew some girls from St. Mary's. When did she go there?" interjected Susan.

"From 1958 to 1962," Helen told her.

"I graduated from Milwaukee Hospital School of Nursing, a good Lutheran Nursing School, in 1964," Susan answered.

Helen continued, "Henry and Dad sat down and figured the farm would not be able to support us and Henry if he had a family, so he would have to get an education unless he wanted to join Walter at Fisher Body. Henry decided he would study Agriculture at UW Madison. The goal was to become a County Agricultural Agent. Because of the work on the farm, he was allowed to commute to school and take a lighter class load. He had planned to graduate in the spring of 1966.

Henry and Katy had the summer together before school started and they made the most of it. Henry wanted to ask her to marry him, but the school rules were that she could not be married or engaged during nurse's training.

Henry worked the farm here with Dad and she went away to school. They wrote often and saw each other when he would drive in to Milwaukee or she would get a weekend off at the farm. She graduated in the fall of 1961. She went to work at Mercy Hospital, the Catholic Hospital in Janesville.

That year for Christmas, Henry gave Katy a diamond ring and they set a date. They wanted a Christmas Wedding in 1962. Then they began to get some help from her family. I don't know why, but Christmas wasn't right. They had to change the date. Then came the ultimatum from the priest! Henry had to take instruction.

We talked to our pastor about this and he was very open minded. He said this would only reinforce the faith Henry was brought up with. Henry agreed to take instruction from the priest if Katy would do the same with our pastor. This was hotly debated in Katy's family and agreed to by Katy. Henry took instruction in the spring. Pastor was right, it only confirmed everything Henry had been taught in his youth. Henry remained a staunch Lutheran. Henry refused to join the Catholic Church.

Then it was Katy's turn. The pressure on her from within her family was so great that she refused to follow through and talk with the Lutheran Pastor. We thought this would be enough for Henry to see that marrying her would not be possible and he should give the idea up.

Yet, after all of this, they were still in love and prayed for something to break the impasse. I guess each in their own way felt their love was strong enough to somehow overcome this obstacle. The one thing that did change was the date for the wedding. There wasn't one!"

"You having a good talk in there?" came Fred's voice from the entryway at the back of the kitchen.

"You done already?" questioned Helen.

"I prepared everything that was ready. That was a little over two acres from the first week's setting," Fred was quick to say.

"Is Henry still sitting under the tree by the fence?" Helen asked, concerned.

"I waved to him and I think he is walking slowly back here now," Fred answered.

It was then that the back door to the entryway slammed and Henry entered.

"Have you got it all thought through now?" Fred asked in a patient, fatherly manner.

"For Pete sakes, give the boy time," Helen told Fred bluntly.

"I better go wash the tobacco sap off me and get changed for supper," Fred was quick to say.

Henry looked at his mom and then at Susan and said, "I have been able to put it past me. Now I have some things I must do right away. Look at what time it is! Susan, will you take a little walk with me? Mom, I think you should start supper a little early today."

Henry walked over to Susan and, taking her by the hand, led her out through the side door.

"Susan, first, I love you and want to be with you."

"Oh, Henry!" Susan cried as she threw her arms around him and gave him a big hug.

Henry continued, "Now we have to decide what to do tonight. I want to stay here with my parents. Will you stay with me or do you have to go home to your folks?"

"I want to stay here with you," she replied enthusiastically.

"Then you better call your folks and explain to them what has happened and that you will be staying. I will tell my folks we will be staying," Henry explained. "Then, after supper, we will spend time with my folks and maybe even with Walter and his family if they come over. This will help you get to know them better. They are all older and will probably go to bed early. Then we can talk."

His flood of words and plans came at her so fast that she stood transfixed, not knowing what exactly to do. Henry broke the spell by taking her by the hand and leading her back into the house.

"Mom, Dad, I know you are not prepared for this, but I want to spend the night and I have invited Susan to stay. We need to call her folks and tell them what has happened, as they are probably expecting us to be back at the farm by now," Henry announced.

"I wouldn't have it any other way, but I have to clean the room and get it ready for you and I have to fix someplace for Susan to sleep," Helen happily answered.

"Don't you worry about a thing. Susan and I can make the bed up in my old room and she can sleep there. I used to do very well sleeping on the davenport in front of the TV in the living room. As far as needing anything else, all we really need is a place to sleep."

"Well, if that is what you want to do I guess it will be okay with me. The sheets have to be changed, as the grandsons helping on the farm slept there last," Helen concluded.

"It is good that you are staying. That will give us a chance to talk," observed Fred. "Susan, the phone is over there on the wall by the door. You probably should call. We don't want to worry your folks."

"We should call Walter and tell him Henry came home," Helen suggested. "He might want to come over and visit."

"I'll try him as soon as Susan gets done talking to her folks."

"I'll go upstairs and change the bedding and get the bedroom ready for Susan," Henry announced as he headed to the stairs and was gone.

Susan continued on the phone for a while and then turned to Helen and Fred after hanging up the phone.

"Mom and Dad couldn't believe that Henry grew up so close. They want to come over and visit you as soon as they can. They would have liked to have come tonight, but I told them Henry is busy catching up."

Fred went to the phone and placed his call to Walter. The phone rang, but nobody answered it. While he was doing that, Helen got busy making supper. This was a traditional Sunday supper that she had been making for years. The meal consisted of boiled rice with cinnamon and sugar, garden fresh vegetables, bread, and cream of corn from the freezer. The beverage was a choice of a glass of water or a glass of milk.

By the time Henry came back downstairs, the meal was almost ready to be served.

They sat around the supper table much more relaxed than they had been at dinner. Fred had a lot of questions for Henry. Henry and Susan did their best to answer them. They shared stories of what had happened during the last two years and were just happy to be together again. Fred was never able to get Walter on the phone, so seeing him would have to wait for another evening. Around eight thirty, Fred suggested getting some rest, so he and Helen needed to turn in for the night.

CHAPTER 16

The "old folks" went off to bed, leaving Susan and Henry alone in the kitchen.

"Come upstairs with me. I want to show you where you will be sleeping and how to find the bathroom," Henry invited.

They went upstairs and he showed her around.

"We aren't going to bed yet?" Susan asked in a surprised voice.

"No, I want you to be familiar with the upstairs so if we stay up late, you won't wake up Mom and Dad when you do go up to bed," he jokingly answered. "Would you come outside? I want you to take a little walk out in the field with me."

"Would this be a romantic walk?" she asked teasingly.

"Probably not that romantic," he answered seriously.

They came quietly down the stairs and went out the side door, making just enough noise so that Henry's mom and dad would know they left the house.

The heat of the day was dissipating and the warm, westerly breeze felt refreshing. The sun was a round orange ball sitting slightly above the treetops, preparing to disappear. He took her by the hand as he led her out to the path and across the field.

"Did you have a nice talk with mom this afternoon?" he asked.

"I asked her a few questions and she ended up telling me the family history."

"Did she tell you about Katy?" Henry asked nervously.

"Are you still in love with her? Is there a chance you might get back with her? I need to know," pled Susan.

"She didn't tell you?" responded a surprised Henry in disbelief.

"Tell me what?" Susan countered.

"Katy is dead," he replied grimly.

"Oh," a stunned Susan muttered. As they walked along, she began to realize that the melancholy that came over Henry when his memory returned was somehow related to Katy and her death. She didn't know what to say. She sensed Katy's loss still deeply affected Henry. *Was there anything she could say to comfort him?* All she could do was to squeeze his hand and walk silently beside him.

Henry said nothing more. He just squeezed her hand and led her along the path that ended at the large tree along the fence line. At the base of the tree, beside the fence, was a spot where the grass had been pressed down by someone sitting there, someone who would have sat there for a long time with his back against the trunk of the tree.

Henry pointed to the spot and said, "Please sit down."

Susan did as he indicated and sat on the spot with her back against the tree.

The sun was dropping behind the distant row of trees. Henry sat cross legged about two feet away, along the fence, facing her and the tree.

She was in shadow in the faint light of the waning moon.

"This is where I always came to meet Katy. This was our special place. You are the only other person I have ever brought here," Henry explained, and before Susan could say anything, he continued, "Katy Collins lived on the farm across this fence. She was the youngest child and had older brothers and a sister who thought she was a pest. I only found out I had an older brother when I was about ten years old. We were both lonely kids. We had this in common. We were the only kids our age at school. She started out being the sister I never had. We became very close. I always knew she was Catholic, but at that age it didn't seem to matter.

In about fifth grade, I think, I started to like her as more than a friend, but it was a secret and I told no one. I spent as much time as possible with her. As you know, living like you did on the farm, farming is a lonely life and after chores were done and before sunset, I would come over to this tree and sit where you are sitting now and daydream. Early on, I told Katy I did this. Soon, every chance she would get she would come to her side of the fence and join me.

This became our special place. We could pour our hearts out to each other. We usually didn't have anyone else to talk to, so it just happened.

I never had any serious girlfriends and she never dated any other boys. Whenever we could we spent time together here."

Susan thought about this for a few moments and said, "I had a lot of friends at church. I didn't have any serious boyfriend, as such. I had some dates in high school, but most of the time there was a group of us who always did things together and we more or less paired up," Susan said coyly, remembering her younger days.

"We had a group at church, the Walther League, where we did things together, but I never got close with any of the girls. In high school, a bunch of us guys chummed around together, but as soon as I could drive, I began dating Katy. We were just natural together. We fit," said Henry.

"When I went through confirmation classes, Katy and I discussed religion for the first time. I was learning what made me a Lutheran and how the Lutherans differed from the Catholics, but when we discussed the different teachings, she mostly agreed with me. All the way through high school, I talked about my faith and she seemed to listen. She never discussed her beliefs with me.

Long about our junior year, we started to get serious about each other. As soon as the class rings arrived, I had hers and she had mine. I think I wore mine only one day. After that, it was either wrapped on the bottom with tape on her finger or on a chain around her neck.

In our senior year, we had to decide what we wanted to do for the rest of our lives. She wanted to be a nurse. I wanted to farm. She was accepted into nursing school at St. Mary's in Milwaukee. I wanted to remain in agriculture. My plans were flexible; hers were contingent on the rules of her nursing school.

I wanted to give her an engagement ring when she left for school, but the school rules forbade it. We came to talk about it at the place where we were most comfortable. We sat on each side of the fence by this very tree and talked it through. It was here we pledged ourselves to each other. We would be married when she graduated. That was our plan.

That summer, we only dated on weekends but almost every night we were not on a date we would say good night right here across the fence. We also began doing more and more things with her family. I had known her older brothers since they moved next door. Now that we were spending so much time together, I became friends with her older brothers.

That fall, she went away to school and we saw each other only when she could get away. The nursing school she attended was run by the Catholic hospital. Not only did she learn nursing, but she learned more about her religion. Whenever religion came up, her responses had changed. At the time, I didn't think anything of it, but her experience with the Nuns seemed to have changed her.

While she was away at school, I farmed with Dad and took classes at the University of Wisconsin, Madison. I would have graduated this year, but I gave it up. I had to change my life." Henry's voice broke as he continued, "I couldn't stay around here any longer. I had to leave."

"What happened?" she asked in a low sympathetic voice.

Henry ignored her question and continued, "We loved each other, we were close, and we planned to get married. When she graduated, she came back here and lived with her mom and dad while she took her State Boards. She got a job at Mercy Hospital and found it convenient to continue living on the farm. I continued to work the farm and go to school.

On Christmas Eve that year, we were celebrating at her house. Her brothers, their wives, and all the kids were there. There was so much activity I almost didn't do it. I wanted to take her somewhere romantic. I wanted to do it privately! I had planned so many different ways to ask her. I couldn't get her alone.

Everybody was opening presents and when it came time for my present to her, the pressure from the family was terrible. Maybe some had guessed what I wanted to do. They all wanted to watch. Her present wasn't under the tree. Everybody was looking at me. I didn't have a secondary present to give her to take the pressure off. I did what I had to do in front of the whole family. I got down on one knee, opened the box I was holding, took the ring from the box, placed it on her hand, and asked her to marry me. In front of her whole family, she excitedly said yes. I wanted my proposal to be more romantic, but things don't always happen the way you plan. I think her brothers expected her to get a ring. Her dad made some comment about not being asked first for his daughter's hand, and her mother thought that this was so sudden. There were also comments to the effect that the wedding couldn't take place until I joined the church. Katy and I pretty much ignored those comments. We hadn't had time to talk, so we gave her family no wedding date. The rest of the evening, her sisters-in-law spent time admiring her ring.

Christmas Day, Katy and I spent with my family. She came over to our place right after late Mass. Right before dinner, Mom noticed the ring on her finger. I had planned to announce our engagement after we ate, but things don't always happen according to plan.

My brother and his family arrived a bit later and Katy had another chance to have more people admire her ring. My family welcomed her with open arms.

When I was alone with Mom and Dad, they were supportive. The only advice they gave was to remember I was brought up Lutheran and I would have to follow my conscience. I would have to live with whatever I did. They gave me no outward pressure to remain Lutheran. Their pressure was more subtle with comments like, 'It's nice when the whole family can go to church together on the Holidays,' or, 'The church will look so nice decorated for the wedding.

My brother was blunt in his comments. He stated that if I wanted him at my wedding, it better be in the Lutheran Church. We had to come up with a wedding date, so after mulling it around for a while, we decided to wait and have a Christmas wedding the next Christmas. This would give us enough time to get a house and make all the necessary arrangements. Her mother was against a Christmas wedding. She didn't say why or offer any alternative dates, but it couldn't happen on Christmas. I continued in school and she continued to work. We were engaged, but that was all. We had no wedding date set and we spent as much time together as possible with her family and mine. That was part of the 'softening them up strategy.' Christmas came and went. We had been engaged for a full year and we still had no wedding date.

During this time, the religion question kept popping up. I didn't want to give up my Lutheran heritage and become Catholic, but I also wanted to marry her. We talked it over. She seemed willing to listen to my side if I would listen to hers. At the insistence of the Priest, I agreed to take instruction in the Catholic faith. She agreed to take the adult course offered by my Pastor. We would set a wedding date when that was done. We would go through instruction together with the Priest in the spring and then in the fall we would meet with my Pastor. This was my understanding of the arrangement. Little did I know that it wasn't the way her family understood the arrangement.

We completed the Catholic instruction in May. At that point, I was expected to join the Catholic Church. That wasn't my plan! At that point, I found out she had only agreed to the original plan to get me into instruction. I still was in love, but I wasn't Catholic. We made plans to go off somewhere and get married anyway, but the pressures around her from her family and the nuns with whom she worked at Mercy Hospital all had an influence on her. I just couldn't accept the Catholic Church and she couldn't accept the Lutheran church. Again, we were at an impasse. Through June and most of July, we were still engaged but were not seeing much of each other. I didn't call her and she didn't call me. We said hi to each other when we met on the street, which was seldom. This probably was the loneliest I had ever been. Here my best friend was, a fence away, and we were not seeing each other. We were hardly talking.

I started again to go sit under the tree by the fence in the evenings after work. I didn't have any classes that summer and the work around the farm was going good, so I did have some time to myself after milking. It was quiet by the tree and I didn't feel quite so lonely. One night when I got there, Katy was sitting with her back to the tree on the other side of the fence. She broke the ice. She asked me if I missed her. I asked the same question of her. We both knew the answer. If we weren't lonely, why were we sitting in our old spots under that tree? I asked her how she had been and she asked me the same question. I learned that the pressure on her to break up with me was intense. She had been lonely too. Her mother was pressuring her to find a more suitable, Catholic, boyfriend. We talked until late into the night that day and we continued to meet by the tree every night she could make it. Nothing was settled and we still had no wedding date."

"You still love her, don't you?" Susan stated in a sad voice.

"I guess she will always have a place in my heart. I think a first love will always be a fond memory locked up where no one will ever find it. I think it is the nature of things," Henry answered stoically. "Do you have a first love locked away somewhere in there?"

Susan pondered that question for a while as if searching her memory for just the right name.

"There was the boy I had a crush on all the way from about fifth grade on through high school. Nobody ever knew. Justin Craig lived in town and I thought he was *it.* Funny thing, though, he never looked at me once. He liked thinner, shorter girls. I never appealed to him. As I said earlier, I had a couple of boyfriends in high school, but I was never serious about any of them. One wrote to me for a while in nursing school, but that didn't last either. There were a group of us in Walther league that chummed around and in nursing school I met some boys at the Gamma Delta meetings, but nothing ever got serious."

"You are such a pretty girl. You should have had a lot of boyfriends," Henry remarked.

"Flattery will get you anything," Susan replied, trying to change the mood. "So did you ever get back together with Katy?"

"By the end of that summer, we were going places together and planning things, but she never did go with me to meet with Pastor and learn about us Lutherans. We started to make our private wedding plans for a June wedding. We chose June 20, 1964 at four o'clock. She got pressure from the church, her parents, and from work, but we decided not to have a church wedding. We would have a simple civil ceremony, invite both families, and welcome whoever would come."

"That sounds like a good compromise," Susan commented. "What happened?"

"We announced it to her mom and dad first and got the expected result. They wanted the blessing of the church and to get this, we would have to be married by the Priest. I wouldn't have to become Catholic to do this. I knew that if I agreed to this, I would have to sign the paper that promised my children would be brought up Catholic. I held my comments back and let that pass. I hadn't agreed to that, but I didn't want to open up old wounds right then. When we were alone, I told Katy I still wanted a Justice of the Peace to marry us. She held her comments and didn't disagree either. We told my mom and dad what we had planned. They thought that that was the best compromise and told Katy they would be happy to get their moping son happily married and in his own house. All in all, I thought things were progressing pretty well.

After Thanksgiving, we rented a hall for the June date in Stoughton for the reception and started to look for the band to play for the dance. As Lutherans, we don't generally promote dancing to our youth, but we decided those coming from her side of the family would definitely dance and my people would do a Polka or Schottische if the band played the right music.

We had a great Christmas time together. She came to Christmas Eve services with my family and I attended Midnight Mass with hers. I thought we had made great strides in working out our difficulties.

We still had not settled the wedding details. Her parents took my non answer about the Priest marrying us as a yes. They had been making arrangements for the wedding to take place in the Catholic Church. Katy and I had been making plans for the civil wedding. It was a snowy, blustery day Friday, January 24th, 1964, a day I will never again forget. Katy and I went out to eat at this bar on Lake Kegonsa just off Highway 51 in McFarland. On Friday's, Katy still liked to follow the Catholic custom to eat fish. I, out of pure German Lutheran stubbornness, would always eat steak. We had a good meal and when we were done eating we left the table and went up to the bar. There, we met Terry and Howard, two of her brothers who had stopped by for a drink after cutting wood on a farm owned by one of their friends. We were standing around the bar drinking beer when some comments were made about the wedding. One word led to another and soon Katy and I were on opposite sides of a question. I don't even remember what the question was."

Susan heard Henry's voice begin to crack and it seemed to her as though he was fighting back a sob.

Henry stopped talking and worked to compose himself before beginning again. "It was at this point her brothers offered to drive her home and she accepted rather than have me do that. We all left the bar together. She went over to her brother's car and got in. She sat in the middle between them. I went over to my car. We left the parking lot and headed south on Highway 51 to Stoughton. There was a shortcut we would usually take that went across to County Road N."

Again, Henry was having trouble telling his story. He had to stop and take a couple of deep breaths before he was able to continue.

"The snow had been falling the whole time we had been in the bar and now was at least four inches deep. I had no trouble driving on it, as I had put the new Goodyear Town-N-Country snow tires on the rear wheels of my car. Terry's car had more trouble getting out of the parking lot and on to Highway 51. His back tires weren't gripping well at all in the new snow. He probably should have put chains on his back tires. Highway 51 was snowy with the new fallen snow covering some of the old icy spots, but there were definite tracks in the snow on the road kept clear by the heavy traffic. We picked up speed as we drove. The cross road we would take was located on a curve and as we approached the curve, Terry didn't slow his car to make the turn."

It now seemed to Susan that Henry would have a hard time continuing to tell his story as his voice sounded more and more strained.

"At the time, I thought it was a good move on his part as 51 was well traveled and usually plowed. To follow it to Stoughton would take us to County Road N the long way to her home. Dane County always plowed N right away. It would be a much safer route. But as Terry rounded the curve, he hit a patch of snow-covered ice. His car went careening off the edge of the road as though it were rocket propelled. The snow bank made by the snowplow along the side of the curve didn't slow the car down, but rolled up under the car, keeping it from nosing into the ditch and slowing. I was far enough behind his car to see what was happening and slowed down immediately, as I knew I would be needed to help. There was one big tree at the back of the ditch on that corner. That was the tree his car decided to hit dead on." At this point, Henry could not go on.

Susan suspected she now knew what happened to Katy. She saw how hard it was for Henry to continue to tell her about this. She didn't know what to do to console Henry, but she wanted to do something. She got up and went the two feet over to where he was sitting, knelt in front of him, and leaned forward, giving him the biggest hug she could.

CHAPTER 17

Susan had changed positions and was now sitting on the grass beside Henry. She could see the deep loss he still felt reflected on his face. She now understood why Henry had hidden his love for her. He needed to keep his secret until he knew who the Katy in his mind was so as not to hurt her. The way he had tried to protect her made her love him all the more. She knew no words to say that would not have sounded trite. The only thing she could do was put her arm around his shoulder and try to comfort him. He responded by putting his arm around her waist, holding her tightly to him. They sat like that for some time and finally he regained his composure enough to continue his story.

"I remember it as though it were yesterday," Henry agonized as he spoke so slowly. "It is so clear. I parked my car in the snow on the right hand shoulder of the road. I left the motor running. I turned on my left turn signal as a warning to the following traffic. The visibility was poor due to the falling snow and I wanted to give any traffic coming around the bend as much warning as possible. I got out of the car and stepped in the deep snow. I was wearing my good Oxford shoes with no boots over them. Immediately, they were full of snow. The warm leather soles were slippery on the ice under the fresh snow. I carefully made my way across the icy road to the other shoulder. By then, another car had come around the curve, stopped, and parked on the shoulder ahead of mine. A man got out of the car and also began to come across the road."

Henry stopped talking and wiped his eyes on the sleeve of his shirt.

"Were there many cars on the road that night?" Susan asked.

Henry looked over at her and gave her a half smile and continued, "For that night I think there were quite a few."

He turned back and, in a trance-like state, looked straight at the tree and continued. "From where I now stood, I could see exactly how the car had hit the tree. It had had enough speed to have pushed the snow banked at the edge of the road under it, lifting it so it didn't hit the ditch, but went right into the base of the tree. The impact area on the car was just to the left of the right headlight, causing most of the crushing to take place on the passenger's side of the car. In some respects, this was good because the bottom of the passenger's-side door was above the snow level in the deepest part of the ditch. At first, it looked as though it would be easy to get the door open. From where I stood, it looked as though the driver's side door would be difficult to open against a lot of snow piled in the ditch."

Again, Henry stopped for a moment to catch his breath and regain control of his voice.

Susan watched him as he did this and thought to herself, *This is why his mother probably thought he would never be able to tell me this story.*

Henry cleared his throat and began again. "At first, it looked like steam from the radiator coming up from under the crumpled hood of the car, but then the steam began to take on a dark, smudgy appearance and I knew there was fire under that hood. I knew I had to act fast.

I waded through the deep snow in the ditch as fast as I could to the passenger's-side door. I reached the door and tried to open it. I was standing in the ditch, snow up to my waist, reaching up to the door handle to try to pull the door open. The metal from the front fender was pushed back against the edge of the door and the door frame must have been sprung. I was at a bad angle and couldn't get the door to budge. The man who stopped joined me at the door. He was standing in a shallower place in the ditch, leaning forward and had better leverage. The fire had begun to roar under the hood at the front of the car. The car was filling with smoke. By this time, there were several more people from cars that had stopped. Several people were working on the other side of the car and had the driver's side door opened a little and were trying to pull Terry out from between the seat, which had moved forward and the steering-wheel post, which was pushed into his chest, pinning him. In the end, it took three of us to get the door open far enough to pull Howard out of the car. Howard was no help. His head had hit the windshield and he was either out cold or dead. By this time, the fire was beginning to consume the inside of the car. We got Howard pulled free and I was trying to climb up on the door sill to get to Katy when someone jerked me back."

At this point, Henry stopped talking. He had an intense look on his face. He was looking straight ahead as though he was again watching the car burn before him, trying to describe what he was seeing.

Susan looked over at him and could see the tears welling up in his eyes again.

"Wasn't it dangerous trying to pull someone from a burning car like that?" she asked, trying to interrupt his thoughts for a moment.

As if in answer to her question, Henry continued having a harder and harder time controlling his voice.

"Moments later, the whole interior of the car became a fireball. They had jerked me away before I would have been badly burned or killed in the explosion. There was nothing more I could have done!" Henry agonized. "I watched from a distance. All I could do was stand there in the cold and falling snow and watch as she burned in the car. It all happened so fast! As soon as they got Terry out, they placed him in a car and rushed him to the hospital. There were no telephones handy, so someone had gone to Stoughton to get the police and a fire truck. When we checked Howard and found he was still breathing, someone else took him to the hospital too. The firemen arrived and began the process of bringing the fire in the burning car under control."

"Shouldn't you have gone to the hospital too? After all, you had been down in the snow and were probably in shock," Susan observed.

"When the police came, they wanted to take me to the hospital, but the car was still burning and I couldn't leave her yet. I couldn't leave her there, at least not then. I stayed until the County Coroner came. There was an ambulance. I don't even know when it arrived. The Coroner took statements from those standing around. The police had been talking to some of the others and they pointed to me. That was when the policeman came over and took my statement. After some time, the firemen had cooled the car enough for them to remove what was left of Katy. I didn't want to be there for that. As I stood there and as the heat from the burning car went away, I realized that I was cold, wet, and shivering. I took my cold and shivering body and sat it in my warm car and realized it was time to leave. I drove right to the hospital. The car was warm enough to have stopped my shivering, but I was still wet. It was ten thirty by the time I reached the hospital. I had to know about Terry and Howard.

By this time, the police had called the Collins family. Paul and Mary were in the emergency room waiting for news on the boys. They had been told Katy died. I told them what I had seen and how I had tried to get Katy out, but it was too late. We stood there in silence for a few minutes. I had said what I needed to say and they hadn't said much in return. I left them when the Priest arrived. He said something about last rites at the funeral home and that was all I heard."

"But you were her fiancé!" Susan exclaimed.

Henry remained silent for a while, looked over at her and said, "We weren't married yet. She was not mine. She was still theirs."

Susan pondered that for a moment and, "Oh," was all she could say.

Henry continued. "I went home. Mom and Dad had already gone to bed and I decided not to wake them. I went right up to bed. I had just lost my best friend, the love of my life, my future wife, and I was in a daze. The morning came and I was up early to milk the cows. I hadn't told Mom and Dad about the accident yet. I think I was still in that dazed state of mind that believed it had been a dream. Maybe I wasn't ready to face her death. Maybe I just didn't want to try to explain what had happened. I don't know how to describe the state of mind I was in. Maybe it was like when you are on automatic and you do things and say things, not realizing what you are doing. We had a radio in the barn. It was always tuned to the local Madison station. It played twenty-four hours a day. We were entertaining the cows, I guess. Anyway, the news came on and the accident was announced. Dad looked at me and asked me if we hadn't gone out to eat as planned. It was then that I broke down and cried. It was at that point my shell broke. Dad told me to leave the rest of the milking to him and go tell mom. He said she should hear it from me before she heard it on the news. The rest of the morning was a blur. I dressed up real warm and walked out to her, to our tree. It had been our place for almost twenty years.

About mid morning, I checked in with Paul. I asked them how they were and if I could help them in any way. They were going to the funeral home at about eleven to meet with the funeral director and make plans. I wasn't invited to go along. They said they would tell me what they decided later. I wanted to be there, but as I was not Catholic, I had no real say in any of the plans. That afternoon, I went to the hospital to see Terry and Howard. Terry had internal injuries and would spend another three days in the hospital. He remembered an awful lot about the accident. He said that the tires on the car were not that old, but when they hit the ice, he had no control of the car at all. He thought Katy was dead before the fire because she had hit the center of the dashboard hard and he didn't see her breath. He told me they had chainsaw gas in the backseat of the car because it wouldn't fit in the trunk and he thought that was what ignited the fireball I described.

I stopped in to see Howard and find out how he was doing. We hadn't opened the door fast enough and he had suffered some burns from the heat on the lower part of his body and would be in the hospital for a while yet. He had been knocked unconscious and remembered nothing about the fire or how we got him out of the car. Sometime Saturday afternoon, Paul called and left the funeral arrangements with mom. Visitation at the funeral home was on Sunday afternoon and again on Sunday evening. There would be a short time for visitation Monday morning at the funeral home before the eleven o'clock Funeral Mass at the Church.

Sunday, I went to church. Many of my friends came up to me and said the things you say to someone who has lost someone. I told them I appreciated their condolences and left as soon as I could. I know they meant well, but it was hard to face them yet. That afternoon and evening were spent at the funeral home with the casket. My mom and dad attended her Funeral Mass at the Catholic Church with me. They usually asked non-Catholics to leave when they begin a certain part of the Mass, but they allowed us to stay. It was a sunny day, but cold. At the graveside ceremony, I only felt the warmth of the sun. After the service, we went next door" to the reception at the Collins' and paid our respects.

Although Katy and I had been engaged for a long time, it was as if I were a stranger there. I talked with Paul and I said some kind words to Mary, but without Katy there with me I felt totally out of place. After the funeral, I tried to put my life back together again. It was so lonely not to have her as a part of me. Even though we were not married, we were as close as many married couples ever get."

The intense look was gone from Henry's face. He seemed calm and slowly began to make a move to get up from the ground. The evening chill was descending on them and the accompanying dew was forming on the grass around where they were sitting.

Susan also began to get up. "I think I have to stretch a little," she said, changing the subject.

"I need to move around too," replied a subdued Henry.

Susan came over to him, put her arms around him, and laid her head on his chest and just hugged him.

"Thank you for bringing me to your special place. I love you. I have loved you for a long time and hoped you loved me too."

Henry put his arms around her and held her tight.

"I have had feelings for you that I was afraid to have. I couldn't act on them until I was free to do so. I love you and want to be with you."

"Oh, Henry," she murmured as she hugged him and gently tilted her head up and kissed him.

Henry found her lips and gave her a long kiss back and then said, "There is still more I must tell you. Would you like to sit down now under my tree and hear it or would you like to wait and do it someplace else?"

"Let's do it here," she answered.

Susan stepped closer to the tree and leaned against it. Henry stood close to her beside the fence and continued his story.

"I finished the winter semester in school and I worked here on the farm. I was so lonesome; I began to spend a lot of time here at the tree. She wasn't here, but many times I felt as though she was. I visited her grave at the cemetery and, at times, I would talk to her there. The Collins's were kind to me, but I had a hard time spending time with them. There were too many memories. At the end of the semester, one of my classmates was getting married and one of the things his bride demanded was that he got rid of his Harley. I swapped my old car for that bike. I guess I really wanted change."

"Your mother didn't like that bike," Susan observed.

"She thought it was dangerous and I guess she was right. Dad didn't like it either, but he wasn't as vocal about it," Henry explained. "I had to change my life. It was too tied up with Katy and the farms. About mid July, I sat down with Dad and had a heart to heart with him. I told him I couldn't take being around the farm and the area. I was going to go find someplace that didn't remind me of Katy. I decided going west would show me the plains and remind me of the farms. I went east. I concluded that going into the mountains would give me new surroundings and a new life. I headed east and Huntingdon was the first place that appealed to me. I saw a help wanted sign for a glass factory and applied. They put me to work right away. I found a boarding house and I poured my energy into working. I worked long hours and the pay was very good. It didn't cost a lot to live. I have a bank account back in Huntingdon, which will pay off some of my debt. I liked riding my bike, but it had served the purpose I bought it for and as fall headed toward winter, I realized I would need a car. I sold the bike for more than my old car had been worth and bought an old Ford in really good shape for very little money.

One day, I decided I wanted to see the fall colors at Breaks Interstate Park in Breaks, Virginia. I had the Saturday off, so on the spur of the moment I got in my car and drove south. Late that night on the road, I thought I saw a shortcut. I took it. The rain became intense and my visibility was down to zero. I should have stopped, but didn't. After all, I was a flatlander and didn't know much about mountain driving.

I don't remember how I missed the curve, but I remember trying to stay on the road. The next thing I remember, I was upside down in the car with my right leg hurting real bad. I felt nauseous and may have even puked." Henry got this faraway look in his eyes again as if he were witnessing the fire all over again.

Susan put her arms around him again and asked, "Are you sure you can tell me this?"

"Susan, I have to get this off my mind. I can't keep it hidden," he confided and then continued, "I tried to get the car door open. Thankfully, it had sprung and would move. Then I smelled gas and I knew I had to get out of there. The gas must have hit something hot, because suddenly there was fire."

Henry stopped again for a moment to compose himself.

"Here I was, disoriented, in pain, and trapped in this burning car. All I could think of was Katy burning to death in the car. The awful sight as she was consumed in that flaming car. Was I about to have the same thing happen to me? The pain in my leg was surreal. As long as I didn't move it, it was fine. But any change of position caused excruciating pain. For a few moments, I laid there, waiting for death. Then the smoke began to fill the car. It also began to get very hot in there. The driver's window was broken, but there was enough glass left so I couldn't escape that way. It was now up to my left leg and my back to force the door. I knew I was going to die in that car, it was just a matter how long it would take!" Again, his voice faltered and he had to stop to get his voice back.

She hugged him and didn't let go.

"I went through agony. I felt fear, pain, and hopelessness. Then panic set in! I didn't want to die! I didn't want to be burned alive like Katy. In some respects, I died right there. My memory failed me."

"When the sheriff took me up to show me the accident scene, he showed me where they found me. I don't know how I ended up there. In my panic, I must have found super human strength that carried me there." Again, Henry's voice broke and his emotion overwhelmed him.

"I think part of my memory died in that fire because I could not face Katy's death, let alone mine. The realization that I was home and the sudden return of those awful memories are still haunting me now."

They stood in silence, hugging each other for a while and then Henry suggested, "I think it is time I walk you through the wet grass back to the house and we get some sleep."

"I am tired. I think that is a good idea. We can come back here in the morning if you want," she suggested.

"You now know the past and now it is forever behind me. I have no reason to ever come back here again. From now on, the past we will remember is the one we will make," Henry proclaimed as he took her hand and led her across the dewy hay field to the house and rest.

CHAPTER

18

Monday morning, John Rockhouse rolled off the davenport in the living room in the house where Henry Warnke grew up. He landed on his back and looked around. It took him a moment to remember where he was. In his dream, he was John Rockhouse in Williamson talking to George Wheeler, trying to explain something he didn't understand. Now he looked around again and recognized where he was. He was home! The confusion slowly cleared and he wondered what time it was. He could see from the light coming through the windows that it was early morning, but he heard no other usual house noises, so he surmised nobody else was up.

It was late last night when they got back to the house, so he didn't bother Undressing. It Was Much More Efficient To Just Plop Down On The Familiar Old Davenport, Find His Old Spot Like He Had Done So Many Times In The Past, And Go To Sleep. Now He Was Paying For It. He Didn't Remember Ever Being So Stiff In The Morning When He Had Slept There Years Before; Then Again, He Had Been Younger. He Made His Way To The Bathroom To Get A Drink And Take Care Of Some Business. He Felt Grungy In His Clothes, So He Splashed A Little Water On His Face To See If That Would Make Him Feel Any Better. It Didn't. He Spotted The Clock On The Buffet In The Dining Room And Noted That It Was 6:42 A.m.

If I Were At Susan's, We Would Be Half Way Through With The Milking By Now. If I Were Home In Williamson, Home In Williamson? This Is My Home. Or Was. I Would Have Overslept, He Thought.

He Walked To The Kitchen And Decided To Just Sit At The Table And Sort This All Out. There Was So Much Of Him That Was Now John Rockhouse, Yet He Knew He Was Heinrich Karl Warnke. *What Do I Need To Do?* He Asked Himself.

His thoughts began to come fast; *First, Susan and I will go back to her farm this morning. I will have to find out what she wants to do. The two farms are close, so getting someone to drive me around shouldn't be a problem. I know I want to get my things and come back here to spend some time. I want to have Susan come back here and meet Walter, but that will depend on what she wants to do. As it is now, I will just have to wait until she gets up.*

Henry got up from his chair and headed for the side door to go out into the cool morning air. He opened the kitchen door and the cool early morning air was refreshing. It was so crisp and fresh, he decided to leave the kitchen door open to let the fresh air in. He opened the screen door and stepped out.

Outside, he looked around at the farm buildings he knew so well. They weren't as he remembered them. In his mind, they were pristine in their red and white paint. This morning, he could see the areas where the paint had peeled away, where the roof shingles had blown away in the wind, and where some of the window panes in the barn had been broken and never repaired. To his eyes, his home farm had begun to look quite shabby and old. Maybe it had looked that bad before he left and he hadn't noticed it. The last two years had taken their toll and changed many things.

He looked across the field at the Collins' farm. It didn't look any better than his dad's. Although he dreaded the thought, he knew he would be expected to go over and pay them a visit. He had said good-bye to Paul and Mary when he left to find his fortune. Now that he was back, it seemed visiting them was a duty he must not shirk.

He walked back to the house and sat on the cold steps at the side door. As he looked over the scene, he felt out of place. He no longer belonged here. He had come back to a place from out of a long lost dream. It had memories and he loved his mom and dad, but he could never come back to stay.

Time passed as he sat deep in thought on the steps. He didn't hear the noise Susan made as she came down the stairs from his old bedroom. As she entered the kitchen, she looked around and through the screen door and saw him sitting outside on the steps.

"Did you have a good night?" she cheerily asked.

Her voice jolted Henry back to the present and he answered, "You could call it that. How about you?"

"Your bed was very comfortable," she laughed. "You looked like you were either asleep or thinking."

"When I got up, I wandered out here to enjoy the morning air," he replied.

She opened the screen door, came out onto the steps, sat down beside him, and stated, "You look very serious this morning. A penny for your thoughts."

Henry looked over at her, smiled, and asked, "What do you need to do today?"

"I probably should go to the farm and at least get a change of clothes, but I want to spend the day getting to know all about the new you. What do you need to do?" she asked.

At that point, they were interrupted by Henry's mom calling through the door.

"What are you two doing out so early? Come on in. I am making breakfast."

Henry looked at his mother and then at Susan and said, "I need to get cleaned up and all my things are at Susan's farm, so after breakfast we should go there. Then we can decide what we want to do."

Susan looked at him and smiling, and offered, "I am hungry. Let's eat breakfast and find out what your mom and dad want to do. They may have plans for us today."

With that, they went into the house to eat breakfast.

Most of Monday flew by. They went to Susan's, then back to Henry's parent's house.

It was particularly hard for Henry to adjust to the return of his old memories. He had adjusted so well to being John Rockhouse. He never realized how much of him changed in the last two years. He had made a new life apart from his past. Now he had his memories, but he was no longer the Henry from his memories. It was as if he had two separate identities. The return of his memory, though, did not erase the almost two years of being John Rockhouse. He had grown. In some respects, he was John Rockhouse with Henry's memories.

And then there was Susan! Now he knew who Katy was, but she was an old ache, a nostalgic memory, a deep pain from the past. Susan was now! Susan was not a Henry memory, but a John Rockhouse experience. Before he was afraid to love her, now she was all he could think of. They had said they loved each other last night. But that was a momentary thing. He had to find a way to tell her again. The problem was when would be the right time? And the bigger question was did she still feel the same way about him in this morning's light? He thought she did, but was he sure?

They drove to the farm in Milton, showered, changed, and packed the things they would need back at the farm in Stoughton. Susan told her family she wanted to spend the last three days of her vacation getting to know his family better. They would be back and forth between the two farms, but would be staying in Stoughton. Her mother seemed quite pleased with the idea.

They got back to the Warnke farm around three in the afternoon. Helen was busy finishing the Monday washing and Fred was out in the field working with the tobacco.

Henry turned to Susan and, in his stiff Prussian way, reached for her hand and asked, "Would you like to sit with me in the shade of the large Elm tree over in the corner of the lawn?"

"That would be nice."

They walked over to the tree and Henry sat down cross legged on the grass. Susan sat next to him, bending her legs under her and covered them with the skirt of her dress.

Henry looked intently at her and reached for her hand and nervously said, "A lot has happened in these last two days."

"Yeah, a lot has happened."

"I remembered and you found out a lot of things about me. We haven't had the time to digest it all. I am still finding it hard. I feel like

I am in the center of a great tornado with all of this swirling around and all I can do is watch."

Susan looked away as if I deep thought, looked back, and said, "I came home and brought my best friend with me, hoping for a nice quiet relaxing vacation. We were driving to Madison and then there was this shock of you knowing exactly where we were and then being introduced to your mom and dad. All this happened so fast! I am getting used to calling you Henry, though."

"Has any of this changed the way you feel about me?"

"No."

Henry paused and continued to look at her as he brought his other hand to also join hers.

"There is something I must tell you," he stammered and continued. "I don't want to sound like a fool and I hope I am not too forward." Again, he stopped as if to catch his breath and rethink what he was going to say. "I told you this last night and I need to tell you again, I love you. I have for a long time." He said this matter of fact and didn't expect her response.

"Oh Henry, yes!" she replied excitedly as she sprang forward hugging, kissing, and knocking him over on his back on the grass.

They were interrupted by Helen calling from the back door, "What are you two doing out there anyway?"

They spent the rest of Monday meeting Walter and his family.

For the last three days of vacation, they visited family and friends. Susan met the relatives and Henry did the same. Henry was torn between taking Susan with him to visit Paul and Mary, but thought the better of it and went alone. During the walk over to their farm he tried to think of the right things to say to them after being away for so long. In the end all he could do was share a few memories of Katy with them, wish them well and leave. That was the saddest part of the trip.

The last day, August 25th, was spent shuttling between the two farms, wrapping up Henry's unfinished business and Susan's gathering old things she wanted to take with her to Williamson.

Henry and Susan decided that they would start their trip home in midmorning, which would allow them to go through Chicago when the traffic would be the lightest. They took great pains in packing what she was taking back with her into the car. Henry also packed many things to take back such as his Birth Certificate and other things to help regain his identity. The packing was done by mid afternoon. While Susan was finishing her packing, Henry and his dad went to Stoughton for Henry to get a check to cover many of his medical bills and get extra cash.

After they left the bank and were getting into the car, Henry asked, "Dad, what do you think of Susan?"

"She seems like a fine girl."

"Do you like her?"

"Why do you ask?"

"I wanted to get your opinion. I have known her almost two years and I have fallen in love with her. I want to ask her to marry me."

"Are you sure you are over Katy?"

"I fell in love with Susan when Katy was only a dark shadow somewhere in my mind, something stopping me from sharing my feelings with Susan for fear I had commitments that would break us up and hurt Susan. Getting my memory back did nothing to change my feelings for her. It freed me to share them with her."

"Have you told her how you feel?"

"I have, but I want to ask her to marry me. Can we stop at a jewelry store so I can buy an engagement ring? I want to ask her before we leave Milton. I will talk to her father first and I want to have the ring."

"I think your mother will approve and I certainly do. Congratulations!"

After Henry made his purchase, his father drove him to the Radke's to be with Susan.

The two had been inseparable for the last three days and the idea of each family having a separate send off wasn't acceptable to either Susan or Henry, so when they announced they would be leaving on Friday the 26th, something had to be done. The Radke's and the Warnke's got together and planned a farewell party for them for Thursday evening.

The first thing Henry did when he got to the Radke's was to go into the entry room and change into his work clothes.

"Henry, why are you putting those barn cloths on? We should be getting ready for the party," Susan said as though scolding him.

"To help your father get the chores done early so he can get ready for the party," Henry said.

"Just don't take too long. I want you in here early too," she explained.

When he was alone in the barn with Bill Radke, a very nervous and almost stuttering Henry began to speak.

"I have known Susan for almost two years now. I have learned to love her. I think she has feelings for me."

"She does seem very fond of you. After all, the last three days she has been staying at your folks' farm with you," he responded laughingly.

"Well, sir, I want to do things right."

"Yes?"

"I mean in good order."

"Yes, yes. Out with it."

Henry stammered and continued, "I want to ask Susan to marry me, and I want your blessing."

"You have it, but if we don't get on with the milking, it will be midnight before we get to tonight's party."

The milking and the chores were done on time and Henry had plenty time to get ready for the party. Susan and her mother were busy preparing the food and it was shortly before the guests began to arrive that Henry, dressed for the party, finally had a moment alone in the kitchen with Susan.

"My, you look lovely in that calico dress. Is that a new one you bought to bring back?" asked a smiling Henry.

"Yes, these are hard to come by in Williamson. I think they are a Midwest thing."

"That's a pretty ribbon in your hair. I like your hair pulled back like that."

"Thank you for the compliment."

"Those are nice shoes you are wearing."

"Henry, you know flattery will get you nowhere! Now you are being ridiculous."

"But as good as you look, you are missing something."

"Is something showing or not on straight?"

"No, everything looks pretty good, but you still are missing something. You are not completely dressed for the party yet."

"Well I can't possibly think of what could be missing!"

"I have something special for the ring finger of your left hand."

At this point, Henry knelt on one knee and opened the box he held tightly in his left hand. "Will you marry me?" he asked as he took her hand and began to slip the diamond ring on her finger.

Susan looked down at her hand and began to sob and through her sobs said, "Yes, Henry, oh yes!"

The rest of the relatives from both families arrived and the festivities began. Although Henry had asked Bill Radke for his blessing, Bill hadn't had time to tell Susan's mom. Once she saw the ring, she was all questions, questions that neither Susan nor Henry had immediate answers for.

Susan's grandparents were very excited and discussed the possibilities of having great grandchildren to spoil.

Helen Warnke had been told by Fred what to expect. When she saw Susan wearing the ring, she gave her a big hug and told her how happy she was to have her join the family.

None of the other relatives seemed the least bit surprised.

After the party, they drove back to the Warnke farm to spend the night.

Early on Friday morning, August 26th, they said good-bye to Henry's mom and dad. They drove to Milton and said good-bye to Susan's family and began the drive back to Williamson.

EPILOGUE

Henry and Susan drove back to Williamson and picked up their lives where they had left off. It was a shock to George and Beth Wheeler when he told them, but he brought his old high school year book and other things which identified him and they tried their best to call him Henry. The first Monday back, Henry took care of as much business as he could. At eight, he visited the sheriff's office and told the sheriff the good news about his memory and established his identity. The next thing he did was to go to the bank and make the name change on his bank account and deposit the money he brought from Stoughton. Now that he had his Social Security Number and was able to be identified, everything went much smoother. He opened a checking account, but it was two weeks before he could write checks. His check from Stoughton had to clear first. He went up to the hospital business office and told them what had happened. He got a couple more days off to handle details such as going to Huntington to find what was left of his belongings and closing out his bank account there. With all the details taken care of, life went on as before, except Susan was making the wedding plans for a Christmas wedding in Wisconsin and Henry began looking for a house to rent in December.

But that is another story.

www.ingramcontent.com/pod-product-compliance
Lightning Source LLC
Chambersburg PA
CBHW070402200726
48294CB00003B/1050
9781960939944